Along Came You

an Oyster Bay novel

Olivia Miles

~ Rosewood Press ~

ISBN 978-0-9995284-1-9

ALONG CAME YOU

First Edition: January 2018

Along Came You

an Oyster Bay novel

Chapter One

Bridget Harper couldn't have asked for a more beautiful day for a wedding. The sun was shining, and the sky was a solid baby blue, interrupted only by a few big, fluffy clouds that rose high over the Atlantic, where the waves lapped at the shore. It was unseasonably warm for late April in Maine, and the flowers had sprung early this year. Tonight, at the reception, it would cool down, but luckily Bridget had the foresight to order heat lamps for the tent that was set up on the north side of the lawn.

The cake had arrived, all three tiers of white confection, and the string quartet would soon set up on the beach, where they would begin playing exactly thirty minutes before the procession, just in case some guests decided to get an early start for a good seat. Bridesmaids and groomsmen were getting ready at the Oyster Bay

Hotel, scheduled to arrive an hour before the ceremony, in time for group photos, and upstairs the immediate family was gathering their wits with the help of a few bottles of complimentary champagne.

Even from the kitchen window where she now stood, Bridget could see the florist putting the finishing touches on the centerpieces—a colorful mix of tulips that matched the bouquets.

Really, she couldn't have asked for a more perfect wedding. Even if it wasn't her own.

Bridget sighed wistfully and craned her neck out the window, searching for her daughter Emma whom Bridget had sent outside with a watering can more than twenty minutes ago, under the orders to water the rows of tulips that lined the wraparound porch of the large house. Many happy moments had been shared on this porch since she was a girl, and despite renovating the upstairs bedrooms to accommodate guests and transforming the attic into two suites, the porch remained intact when she converted her childhood home into an inn last fall, aside from a fresh coating of white paint, that was. In the winter, she roped garland all around it, and in the spring, the tulips sprang in abundance.

Bridget looked farther down the side of the house and saw Emma crouched down to pick one of the cherished flowers, which she added to the bunch she clutched in her fist.

"Emma!" Bridget hurried to open the window, her heart starting to pound. Guests would be arriving in just a couple of hours, and the last thing she needed was for half the landscaping to be ripped out before the cars pulled up the gravel driveway. She poked her head out, calling again. "Emma!"

Emma froze mid-task, her eyes turning round. Without being told, she picked up the watering can and came inside through the kitchen door, her mouth drooping into a frown.

"Emma, I asked you to water the tulips, not pick them!" Bridget looked in dismay at the stems her daughter clung to. There must have been at least ten flowers. She could only hope they didn't all come from the same patch, but she didn't have time to check, and what good would knowing do? There was nothing she could do now. She still had to shower and change and oversee the vendors and guests, all of whom would be arriving soon.

"I picked them for you, Mommy. I wanted you to have a tulip bouquet, too. Like the bride." Emma's eyes filled with tears nearly as quickly as Bridget could pull her in for a hug.

"Oh, sweetheart." Maternal guilt weighed heavy as she stroked Emma's long, sandy blond hair. "I'm sorry I snapped. I just have so much to do." She sighed as she walked to a cabinet and pulled out a mason jar, which she filled with water. "They're beautiful. Just don't pick anymore, okay? The yard needs to look beautiful, too."

Emma nodded dutifully. "I only picked the best ones."

Bridget couldn't help but smile. What was done was done. A few missing flowers in the yard couldn't be much worse than last week, when she'd washed the guest towels with Emma's white skirt, which happened to contain a red crayon in the pocket.

Turning this home into an inn certainly had its challenges, she was learning. But it was also a dream come true. Without the business, she and her younger sisters would have lost the house when their grandmother moved into a retirement home last year. With its multiple fireplaces and bright, big kitchen, she hated the thought of losing it, or selling it to someone who wouldn't cherish it the way the Harper family did. Now she didn't have to worry about that. She only had to worry about things like running out of soap, because she didn't account for how many guests would pocket one on their way out the door…

"Why don't you put these on the dresser in my room?" Bridget carefully handed Emma the jar of flowers and opened the door to their living quarters: a small sitting room, two bedrooms, and a bathroom that used to be a large family room and a butler's pantry. "I'd put them on the kitchen table, but the caterers—"

Bridget felt herself pale. The caterers. She glanced at the clock on the wall, confirming her fears. The caterers should have been here an hour ago to start prepping for the cocktail hour. In two hours more than fifty guests would descend upon the inn, and, after the short ceremony, would be eagerly awaiting food and drinks.

The bride's father—owner of the *Oyster Bay Gazette*—would certainly not be shy in giving bad press if this wedding were anything but a success.

With a shaking hand, Bridget scrolled through the list of contacts on her phone until she found the number for the catering company. It rang four times before she got through. Sweet relief.

"Hello, this is Bridget Harper at the Harper House Inn. I just wanted to confirm you'll be arriving soon?"

"I was just about to call you, Ms. Harper," the man said, and Bridget's heart officially began to drum so loudly in her chest, she was sure it could be heard through the phone. Nothing good could follow that statement. "Our truck broke down on the way back from a morning event. We're more than an hour away."

More than an hour away. She closed her eyes and pinched the bridge of her nose. This couldn't be happening. With less than six months under her belt, this opportunity was her chance to put the inn on the map, not unravel it.

"We will be there with plenty of time to prepare the dinner," the man continued.

"But! The cocktail hour starts at five!" Bridget's voice was shrill. Even shriller than the time, two weeks into renovating the attic, a pipe leaked and damaged the ceiling of a guest bedroom below.

"We'll be there in time for the dinner," he said again. "I'm sorry, but it's the best we can do."

Bridget hung up the phone and opened the fridge, staring at the ingredients that had been ordered specifically for the event. Crab meat. Lobster. Every kind of cheese and vegetable she could think of.

This wedding was the biggest opportunity she'd been given since opening just before Christmas. Her chance to show that she was a serious business owner, that she hadn't been a fool to give up a somewhat stable career as a real estate agent to take on this huge house and try to make something of it for herself and her daughter. Anything that would go wrong today would be a reflection of her capability, a direct impact on her future. On Emma's future.

She could just picture tomorrow's scathing front page declaring hungry guests and an incompetent staff. She'd be out of business by June.

"Bridge?" Bridget turned to see her middle sister, Margo, peering at her. "You okay?"

She wasn't okay, not in the slightest, but she couldn't risk letting on in case a guest, or worse, the bride's father, happened to pass by and overhear.

"Do you have time to help me in the pantry?" It was cramped but big enough for two. And it had a door. They could talk in there, privately.

Margo's brow furrowed. "I'm swamped at the front desk. You wouldn't believe how many people are calling for last minute reservations, and the bride's family keeps asking for more champagne. And then there's the guest in Room Four." Margo rolled her eyes. "He keeps complaining about the noise. Said there is too much laughter going on. Well, I'm hardly going to tell everyone to keep it down. It's a wedding!"

Bridget barely absorbed a word of Margo's speech. She glanced into the hall and whispered, "The caterers are late. They won't make it in time for the cocktail hour. I don't know what I'm going to do."

Margo's eyes widened, but only for a moment. She tapped the phone in Bridget's hand. "You're going to call Abby, that's what you're going to do."

Abby. Their youngest sister. Abby, who might still be in bed right now, or at the very least in her pajamas, because it was Saturday, never mind that it was nearly two o'clock.

"She made that beautiful pie for the Fall Fest pie baking contest," Margo reminded her. "And Mimi is always talking about the treats she brings to Serenity Hills."

That was all true. And, Bridget supposed that at the very least, she'd be an extra set of hands. Still.

Bridget looked Margo square in the eye. Margo was right. She had no choice. She would call Abby.

And say a prayer.

*

Abby stared at the notebook spread out in front of her, trying to drum up an ounce of enthusiasm and failing miserably. Office assistant—snore. Waitress—been there, done that. Dog groomer—she wanted to take them all home, or least get a dog of her own, which her landlord wouldn't allow. Lifeguard, shampoo girl, manicurist. Check, check, check. She'd tried everything and nothing had held her interest for more than a few months.

There you go, she thought, brightening. Don't look at this as a prison sentence. Look at it as a few months of your life, a way to get back on track, or at least a way to keep the lights on.

With that little pep talk over with, she flipped over the notebook and went to the stove to boil some water for tea. There was an Alfred Hitchcock movie marathon starting in twenty minutes, and she planned to settle onto the couch for the remainder of the day with a bag of cookies. As the kettle began to whistle, her phone began to ring, vibrating in the pocket of her bathrobe.

She pulled it free, surprised to see her oldest sister's name on the screen. Bridget had been busier than ever before since turning their family's home into an inn, and Abby heard from her less and less these days. She knew that Bridget and Margo still talked most days, but that's because Margo was an interior designer who had overseen the design of the guest rooms and lobby, and Abby didn't have anything to offer other than taking Emma to the movies to get her out of the dust-filled house when bathrooms were being installed and floors were being sanded.

And then there was the fact that Bridget and Margo just clicked. Always had. Especially since Margo moved back to Oyster Bay last fall.

"Bridget?" For a moment, Abby worried that something had happened to their grandmother. Mimi's health wasn't what it used to be, and it seemed to be on a downward slope, despite the care she received at Serenity Hills—the nursing home she now lived in, partially against her will. Abby made a silent promise to visit her tomorrow night. She'd bake her some brownies to lift her spirits. She'd even bring something for Pudgie, that spoiled cat she'd bought for Mimi out of guilt. Something that might keep the darn thing busy and out of trouble. "Everything okay?"

"I need your help, if you're free."

"Free as a bird!" Abby said, before remembering that Bridget tended to frown on declarations like that. It tended to make her recite all her "responsibilities" which ranged from packing school lunches for Emma to making sure field trip forms were signed, to doing laundry.

Honestly! Did Bridget think that Abby didn't do laundry? She might not always fold her clothes, but they were clean…or clean enough. Also, she'd learned that if you just hung up your shirt while you showered, the steam worked wonders at loosening the wrinkles. Mostly.

"Need me to watch Emma?" She was Bridget's backup babysitter and loved playing with her little niece. Their favorite thing to do was have a spa day, where they'd do each other's hair, and paint each other's nails, and put on face masks. And there was always glitter. (Even if Bridget called glitter "messy".)

"Ryan's coming by to get her soon," Bridget said, referring to her ex-husband. "Actually, I was hoping you could help me in the kitchen. The Carrington wedding is today. In two hours, actually. And, well, we have a problem. The caterers are running late and we have all these hors d'oeuvres to prepare…" Bridget trailed off, but Abby had heard all she needed to hear.

Cooking! Baking! She was already shedding her bathrobe. "I'd love to help!"

"Really?" Bridget sounded more uncertain than relieved.

Abby balked. As if she'd pass up an opportunity to do what she enjoyed most. Her brownies were a sensation down at the old folks' home, and she had a stack of recipes she was burning to try…once she had a job and could afford the ingredient list. Really, did there always need to be so many ingredients?

"I'll be there in ten minutes," she said, flicking off the burner and running out the front door so fast, it wasn't until she reached for her key to lock up that she realized she was still wearing her pajamas.

*

The kitchen was bustling when Abby arrived a rather shocking nineteen minutes later. Considering she didn't own a car, she must have pedaled with all her might to get here from the center of town where she lived.

Bridget felt her hesitation relax. That *was* rather nice of her sister.

"Shoot," Bridget said. "I forgot to ask if you had a black dress. Well, you can borrow one of mine."

Abby frowned, and looked down at her jeans and tank top. "A dress?"

"For passing out the hors d'oeuvres." Bridget studied a recipe card in her hand, cursing under her breath when she realized that while the item was the same, this particular recipe called for extra ingredients than had been on the caterer's list.

"Passing out the hors d'oeuvres?" Abby's frown was deep. "I thought—" Her cheeks turned pink as she looked over at Margo, who was also inspecting a recipe card with a pinched mouth.

"I know this is the same thing the caterers were going to make, but my recipe is calling for chives, and I don't have chives!" Margo shook her head in frustration.

"Mine is asking for mustard seed," Bridget commented. "I don't think we have any of that in the pantry."

"Let me see," Abby said, reaching out a hand to take the cards. She inspected the lists and the ingredients they had spread out on the counter.

"Bridget, you're fine without the mustard seed, and Margo, you can substitute with onion, which I'm sure you have."

Bridget blinked. She couldn't remember the last time her youngest sister had such confidence!

"Is this all you need to make?" Abby asked. There was something in her eyes. Defiance. Maybe a little hurt, too.

"No. There's a lot more." Bridget nudged Margo, who passed her the menu for the wedding.

Abby studied it silently for a moment. "The brie bites need to go in first, followed by the bacon-wrapped dates. That way the brie can set while the others are baking— you don't want to serve them too warm and have them drip down someone's silk dress."

Bridget glanced at Margo, whose eyes were round.

"I can help with the food," Abby said, her mouth tight. "Or I can go put on that dress you mentioned."

"Help," Margo cut in. She glanced at Bridget, her eyes pleading but firm. "We need all the help we can get."

Abby grinned as she pushed up her sleeves and walked to the sink to wash her hands. "Then scoot aside, and let me do the crab puffs and the brie bites. If you haven't worked with pastry before, best to leave it to me."

Bridget didn't know if it was the tone of Abby's voice, or the way she seemed perfectly comfortable in the kitchen, but she did as she was told and moved to the left. She stood for a moment, in borderline awe, as Abby quickly pulled the ingredients she needed from the fridge and wasted no time getting to work.

Maybe she'd underestimated her sister, she thought. And with the clock ticking away the minutes until the ceremony started, she could only hope so.

*

Bridget had to hand it to her sister. Abby had pulled it off. More than once during the cocktail hour, she had overheard a guest compliment the mini quiche, crab cakes, and bacon-wrapped dates.

Now, as votive candles flickered and then faded, and the guests dwindled, Bridget breathed a sigh of relief. The wedding had been a success, from the weather to the band to the cutting of the cake. The caterers had arrived in time to prepare a delicious three-course meal. From the guests' perspective, it had all gone off without a hitch.

"Champagne, miss?" A waiter from the catering company held a tray of crystal flutes up to her. "Last call."

Last call. Meaning she could finally go inside and flop into bed. Or she might have done, if she didn't have a house full of guests and a kitchen that would need cleaning before breakfast tomorrow.

The caterers were cleaning up most of the kitchen, she reminded herself. And Margo was spending the night to help out with the guests. Maybe she could sneak into the bath with her latest J.R. Anderson novel—a small bit of escapism she looked way too forward to every night.

"Aw, go on," a deep voice behind her urged.

She turned, startled when her eyes met a deep-set stare with a hint of mischief, and a smile that had no doubt been mastered over time. Flustered, she looked away, but there was nothing to look at. Well, unless you counted an empty tent and a waiter trying his best to suppress a smile.

"I shouldn't," she said, daring to look back at him. Cute. Too cute, if experience had taught her anything.

She stayed firm. She had breakfast to think about tomorrow, after all. Usually she liked to get a start on that at night, so she wasn't scrambling in the morning. Even though it was simple—pastries from Angie's Café and fresh, seasonal fruit—she liked to make sure everything was accounted for in advance, especially on nights like this when she had a full house.

The man swiftly plucked two glasses from the tray and held one up to her.

Well, if he was going to insist...

"Thank you." She smiled up at him, wondering why she hadn't seen him earlier. With his dark hair and chiseled features, he wasn't easily missed. But then, she'd been busy, and romance, the real kind at least, had been the last thing on her mind for years.

Still. He was very, very cute.

He tapped his glass to hers, his eyes never straying as he leaned his back and took a sip. She did the same, minus the eye contact part. She wasn't good at that, never had been. Didn't flirt, even when she was young. Now, it felt particularly foreign. She felt old in her mid-thirties, and she was, well, a mother.

God, he was still staring at her. Rattled, she took another sip of the drink. The champagne was cold and bubbly. "I needed that," she confided.

He grinned. A nice grin, of course. Faintly lopsided, but sincere, and the corners of his eyes crinkled. "I had a feeling you did. I don't think I ever saw you sit down."

He'd noticed her. She took another sip from her glass to hide her smile, and then realized if she kept at this she would end up tipsy before long.

Come to think of it, she suddenly did feel tipsy, even though she'd only had three sips. It was the smile. And the eyes. And the fact that he was standing there at all. Men didn't approach her. She'd grown up with all the guys in town and they all knew her ex, of course. Oyster Bay was small that way. Comfortable, but…limiting in its options.

"All part of the job," she said with a smile. "Now the bride and groom can live happily ever after."

Wait. Was that a snort he just gave? From the cock of his eyebrow, it most definitely was.

"Not a romantic?" She couldn't help but feel disappointed, which she knew was perfectly ridiculous because he had only offered her a glass of champagne. He hadn't bought it. And besides, she was a mother. She was hardly in the market.

"More of a realist," he replied evenly, but his mouth twitched. "Fifty percent of marriages end in divorce."

Yes, and she was one of the statistics. Married at twenty-three. Divorced a few years later. A single mom to a one-year-old baby when other girls her age were laughing over Cosmos at the bar with friends and still dating around. It hadn't always been an easy road. In fact, up until a few months ago, it had been downright rocky. Between taking care of her grandmother and two younger sisters and of course her daughter, *and* trying to balance a career, there was no time for romance. No desire, either. Still, weddings always got to her, she couldn't help it. It gave her a feeling of hope, and it was a good reminder that even though her marriage hadn't worked out, love was still out there...for some.

"Don't tell me you're a divorce attorney," she said, noticing suddenly that the last of the catering staff had disappeared and she was alone with this strange man. It was an unsettling feeling, if not entirely unpleasant. Foreign. Usually the only men she was left alone with were Frank, the handyman, and her ex-husband, Ryan.

"Not an attorney, but an expert nonetheless, you might say."

Now she was curious. "Marriage counselor?" She frowned. "But then you'd have to somewhat believe in the longevity of the union, right?"

"Not unless I'd seen how it usually turns out." He laughed. "No, consider my experience...firsthand."

Meaning personal. Well, they had something in common then.

Knowing better than to push, Bridget took the opportunity to reach down and slide the strap of her shoe off her burning heel. It was that or drop into a chair, and she feared if she did that she might never get up again.

"How about you? You really believe in all this fairy-tale

stuff?"

Bridget looked down at one of the remaining centerpieces that hadn't been snatched up by guests and smiled. The flowers were a beautiful burst of color, like happiness tied up with a bow. She nodded once, before looking the man in the eye. "I do."

"And why is that?" he asked, his brow furrowing slightly.

Bridget hesitated. She hadn't had a man look this intensely at her since last month, when a guest informed her in no uncertain terms than he liked a good firm wake-up call, at four o'clock sharp, and despite her desire to protest, she knew from the set of his brow that she had no choice but to comply, and set her own alarm that night too.

"What's wrong with a happy ending?" she said, thinking of her stacks of books piled high on the shelves in her bedroom. "Boy meets girl. Boy falls in love. It's the oldest story in the book."

"Rather stale then," the man replied.

Stale? She looked down at her glass. He was a bit of a grump, wasn't he? An attractive grump, but still...

"Oh, I wouldn't say that. More like...timeless." She gave him a sidelong glance. "Why, can you think of a way to shake it up?"

"As a matter of fact, I can," the man said, his mouth curving into a slow grin.

Before she could react, he set his glass down, stepped

forward, and grabbed her at the waist, pulling her against his chest in one, effortless motion.

And then...he kissed her.

Chapter Two

Well! That had been reckless. Imagine if one of the guests had seen her. Imagine if the father of the bride had seen her! Wouldn't that have made all her efforts pointless?

She'd slipped. Behaved unprofessionally at best. Let her guard down. And she never let her guard down. She couldn't. As a single mother she had to be ready at all times, armed with schedules, and plans, and backup plans, with a bag of snacks in her handbag and an extra set of play clothes in the car. She had to be organized and diligent, and now, as a business owner, all that was doubled.

So what had she been thinking, letting that man kiss her, when she should have been overseeing the caterers and the clean-up, and maintaining a professional image?

She hadn't even caught his name. He'd simply kissed her, left her breathless, and then, with one slow grin, walked away, into the night, leaving her with a slack jaw and goofy smile on her mouth.

Right. First things first. No more goofy smile. She pinched her lips. Tight.

Bridget stood at the kitchen sink, staring out the window onto the stretch of lawn that met the sea. A few guests she recognized as brother and sister-in-law of the bride were sitting in the white-painted rocking chairs that she'd set along the porch, sipping their coffee and talking in low voices. The house was otherwise quiet, meaning most people had chosen to sleep in, no doubt feeling the effects of one too many glasses of wine.

Bridget decided to take advantage of these fleeting minutes of peace by making herself a second cup of coffee. She was just settling in at the old farmhouse table, one of the few pieces she'd kept from the original home, when Margo poked her head around the kitchen door.

Unlike herself, her sister was fresh-faced and perky looking, whereas Bridget felt like a wet blanket, despite her earlier shower. She could attribute it to the stress of the event, but she knew all too well that it was because she'd lain awake all night thinking about the mystery man who had kissed her, replaying it over and over in her mind until it actually felt more like a dream than a memory.

"You heading out soon?" Bridget asked. Margo had selflessly offered to stay the night on Emma's bottom bunk, even though she probably would have preferred to go home to Eddie, her boyfriend and the main reason she had chosen to stay in Oyster Bay after her divorce last year.

Yep, that's how it went. Some people got divorced and then found love again. Whereas others...

Others waited eight years to be kissed again.

"I'll stick around until the guests check out," Margo said. "Besides, don't shoot the messenger, but Room Four called down again." She gave Bridget a knowing look.

"Already?" Bridget stifled a sigh. "What is it this time, because he can't possibly say the house is too loud right now."

"Now he is wondering if there is room service."

"Did you tell him that breakfast is served daily in the dining room?"

"I did. He didn't seem pleased. He also said he hoped the inn would be a bit quieter today."

"It should be. They're all checking out today or tomorrow," Bridget said as she pushed back her chair.

"Wrong. Everyone is checking out by tomorrow, except Room Four. He's here for two weeks." Margo's eyebrows shot up.

"Two weeks!" Bridget hadn't noticed that reservation come through. She supposed she'd been too wrapped up with the first big event her inn had ever hosted. "He wasn't a guest at the wedding, then?"

Margo shook her head. "I guess not. I must have checked him in, but there was so much commotion, I don't even remember him."

"Probably an old curmudgeon with too much time on his hands," Bridget said, and then immediately regretted it. He was a paying guest, after all. A complaining paying guest, but still a guest.

"Probably," Margo agreed.

Bridget started a fresh pot of coffee. "You didn't talk to him when he checked in?"

"There was so much going on yesterday that I must have, but I don't remember. Between the vendors coming in and the wedding party calling down, and the check-ins, I barely gave anyone a solid ten seconds of my undivided attention."

Bridget frowned. A two-week stay in Oyster Bay? Who was this guy?

*

Jack Riley stared at the blinking cursor on his computer screen, trying to summon up some spark of inspiration. Something that would trigger a scene to play out in his mind, a domino-effect of ideas that would fall in line, one building on the next.

As usual, he came up blank.

He reached up and closed the laptop, almost as angry at himself for giving up as he was for wasting another two hours staring at a white page.

What he needed was a shower and a strong cup of coffee. The woman at the front desk had vaguely mentioned something about pastries and fruit in the dining room, that was when she wasn't interrupted by a florist and then a wedding cake delivery.

The festivities were over, at least. Thank God for small miracles. Now he could finally get some peace and maybe a little work done.

Or maybe, if his recent track record said anything, not.

After all, he was supposed to write ten pages last night, at the very least, and instead he'd kissed a random woman. The wedding planner, it would seem, from the way she was walking around the event, surveying everything with a creased brow and a worried look to her eye. He'd watched her, intrigued, deciding that the heroine in his story needed to be a bit more anxious than he'd originally planned.

Yes, that was it. An anxious heroine. He opened his laptop, determined. Stared at the cursor. Then closed the computer shut. Firmly. He had no location, no setting. No inspiration. Definitely no plot. In the past that would come to him, bit by bit, as naturally as scenery unfolded on a long drive. Now it seemed impossible to think that there had been a time when he actually had a story to tell, let alone one he believed in.

He stood. No use sitting here when he was like this. He'd go downstairs, get some breakfast, and then…then he'd write a chapter. Chapter one.

No more distraction today. And no more kissing strangers either.

Though it had been a nice kiss, as far as those things went. He grinned. Still, it was just a kiss. A lapse in judgment. A whim. He was fired up, maybe even a little emotional. That wedding, on the beach, with the white tents…it stirred something up in him, and not in the way he had hoped. He'd gone down there because the noise was so bad; he saw no other choice but to join the fuss, even from a bit of a distance. He thought he might get inspired, find one small thing that gave him a spark. Instead, it made him nostalgic. It made him angry. It made him want to banish every memory of a time and place from his mind, when he was young, and dumb, and another person.

And then he had to see that woman. The pretty one with the blond hair. And she was something to watch, a character study at first, but then, a person of interest. And then…a mistake.

Weddings got under his skin about as much as wrapping up this six-book contract he was tied to did. But this was it, the last book. And then…Well, the future was wide open, wasn't it? No ties. No commitments.

It should be a happy thought. Instead, it just depressed the hell out of him.

Right. No more thinking about any of this! He'd go downstairs, get some breakfast, and then…Chapter One. Nineteen to go. Let the countdown begin.

*

The phone started ringing as Bridget started filling a new basket with croissants. In case it was Ryan saying he needed to coordinate a different drop off time for Emma than originally planned, she stopped mid-task and walked to the kitchen island to check the screen. Her heart sank at the words on the screen. It was her grandmother, calling from Serenity Hills. Mimi tended to call in the mornings, eager for company, and when Bridget didn't answer, she made the rounds, calling Margo and then Abby, and if they didn't pick up, trying Bridget again.

Bridget poked her head into the dining room. The pastry baskets were still half-full, meaning she could steal a few minutes before seconds were in order. Margo was upstairs, tending to the guest rooms, when really where Bridget could use the help right now was with breakfast.

"Good morning, Mimi!" She always tried to keep her voice chipper with her grandmother, even when Mimi could get rather sour, often blaming Bridget for "dumping her" in Serenity Hills to begin with, even if this house had become far too much work for her and she sometimes mixed up the names of her three granddaughters, and once thought Emma was Bridget, still only eight years old.

"Not much of a good morning for me," Mimi sniffed. "But it sounds like everything is peaches for you."

Ah, one of those days. Best not to feed into it, even if the guilt would gnaw at her for the rest of the day.

"Busy as usual. It's the breakfast hour, and soon it will be check out." Bridget walked to the coffee machine to start a new pot. "What do you have going on today?"

"Oh, Pudgie and I might go down to the cafeteria soon. See what slop they're offering today."

Bridget managed not to laugh. The food at Serenity Hills was actually quite good, but try telling Mimi that. "I didn't realize they allowed cats in the dining room," she said.

Mimi paused. "Oh, they don't. But…I have my ways."

Bridget could only imagine what they were. She smiled as she dropped a fresh filter into the machine and began measuring the coffee grounds. The smell was so inviting, she decided to treat herself to another cup. She deserved it, after all; a little reward for yesterday.

Well, not *all* of yesterday, she thought with a frown.

"Why are you frowning?" a voice across the room whispered, and Bridget jumped at the sight of Abby standing in the doorway.

Blinking in confusion, she checked the clock. It wasn't even nine yet and Abby was not only dressed but out and about? It was a running joke, after all, that Abby not only liked part-time work, but the afternoon shift.

"Mimi, I'll call you back this afternoon. Be sure to get outside and have some fresh air. Pudgie loves it," she added, for encouragement. Mimi might not be very willing to take care of herself these days, but she'd do anything for that ornery cat, so he couldn't be all bad, even if he was known to hiss and occasionally scratch, especially Margo, whom he had taken an almost instant disliking to.

She hung up the phone and looked at her sister. "This is a surprise! What brings you by? Did you need something?"

Abby's grin seemed to falter, but only for a moment. She shrugged. "Oh, just seeing if *you* needed any more help with the clean up!"

Bridget stared at her sister, wondering if she was still dreaming. Abby didn't get out of bed before nine, and she certainly didn't offer to help clean up.

She looked around the sparkling kitchen, which she'd scrubbed last night after coming back inside, her knees still shaking from the impact of that kiss, unable to sleep, so she'd put herself to good use instead.

"I think I'm good," she said. "But thanks!"

"Or...did you need any help with the pastries?" Abby looked at the island, where white bakery boxes from Angie's that were delivered each morning sat open.

"Well, you can finish adding some croissants to that basket if you want." Bridget turned back to the coffee machine. Something was up. Something was definitely up.

She set the coffee to brew and walked over to the island, to start another basket of muffins—the guests loved Angie's blueberry muffins, and they were a staple on her menu at the inn, where she was always happy to point out that Maine blueberries were the best of the best.

She worked quickly and picked up the basket to carry it out to the dining room, but Abby chose that time to say whatever it was she had actually come to say. Because she certainly hadn't come to help clean the kitchen or load croissants into a basket.

"So everyone seemed to like the food last night?"

Bridget turned to properly face her sister. She owed her a hug, but her hands were full. Really, she owed her more than that. She owed her coffee. Or dinner. Or…a gift card. "They loved the food, Abby. I didn't realize you knew quite so much about cooking!"

"It's just a hobby really…" Abby's cheeks flushed.

Bridget smiled and turned to go into the dining room to greet her guests, but Abby said, "I'm hoping to turn it into something more, though."

Bridget wished they could have this conversation later, but she owed her sister for saving the day yesterday, and so, with more patience than she felt, she nodded. "You should pursue it, then!"

"I've been thinking that maybe the guests would enjoy a warm breakfast sometimes. Or lunch? Although, I suppose they are all out and about during lunch." Abby shook her head.

Bridget blinked. She could hear a guest grumbling about there not being any more croissants in the basket and another complaining that the coffee was almost gone.

"Mind grabbing that pot of coffee?" she asked Abby. She lifted the giant basket, to show her hands were full at the moment.

"Of course!" Abby's green eyes went round as she hurried across the kitchen to grab the now full pot from the burner. As she walked back toward the entranceway to the dining room, she said, "I was thinking a nice quiche. I make a really good goat cheese and roasted tomato quiche. Or...I mean, I could always share the recipe instead."

Now another guest was complaining about the coffee. Bridget jutted her chin to the dining room and motioned for Abby to follow her.

"Or baked French toast. Oh! Banana Foster French toast. I've brought that for Mimi sometimes and the other residents just follow the smell of cinnamon and come into her room..."

What was her sister talking about? Bridget plastered a smile on her face as she entered the dining room, where the fathers and mothers of the bride and groom were sitting at the large dining table, frowning. "Coffee and croissants!" she announced cheerfully, setting her basket down on the large buffet.

"Are there any more of those blueberry muffins?" the bride's sister asked. Bridget noticed that she already had one on her plate, but who was she to judge? The sister had also pouted through the entire ceremony, clearly not happy to be the older and still single sister. She sympathized.

"I'll be right back with those," Bridget said with a wink.

Abby was quick at her heels on her way back into the kitchen. "I was thinking I could come up with a menu for the week. Maybe do something really special on the weekends. Oh, and seasonal foods! You know, lots of apple offerings in the fall and spices around the holidays."

Bridget stared at the bakery boxes, calculating how much was left. She hadn't counted on the guests having such a hearty appetite this morning. She loaded everything into a big wicker tray. It would just have to do. She'd bring in more yogurt and fruit on her next trip.

"I just thought it might take some of the pressure off of you," Abby continued. "And it might really add something to the business, too. I know that Margo helped with the interior design, and of course you run the place, but, well, I grew up here, too, and I was just hoping to be a part of it."

"Of course. This is always your home, Abby!" Bridget gave her a reassuring pat on the shoulder and hoisted the tray off the counter as she walked back to her guests.

"So then...this will work for you?"

Bridget opened her mouth to ask Abby what she meant, but no sound came out. There, standing in the center of her dining room, with bedraggled hair and a casual T-shirt that hinted at a perfectly sculpted chest underneath, was the man.

The man. The man who had kissed her.

The man who was, by all appearances, her guest.

"So we have an agreement?" Abby was asking.

Bridget's mouth felt like she had just chewed cotton balls. She blinked, staring at the man, wondering if it was too late to run and hide. Should she ignore him, pass the basket off to Abby and bolt out the back door? Or confront him, smile, see if he had spent the entire night thinking about her the way she had so pathetically done about him?

He turned, and oh, God, in the light of day he was even more handsome than she'd remembered him. Piercing blue eyes and a strong, straight nose, and just enough stubble on his jaw to make her want to feel it scuff her cheek.

His eyes widened slightly before he gave her a boyish, lopsided smile, and oh, if her stomach didn't roll over.

"So that works?"

Abby was still talking, and Bridget needed that to stop. "Fine," she said. "Fine."

But everything wasn't fine. She'd kissed a guest. Fantasized about a guest. And now...now she could officially stop thinking it could ever happen again.

Chapter Three

Jack stared at the woman standing in the kitchen doorway, her eyes round, the tray of pastries tipped precariously to the left. Her blond hair was down, loose at her shoulders, and the black dress was replaced with jeans and a blouse, but there was no denying it was the woman from the wedding last night.

"Hello," he spoke first, gauging the mood. "We meet again." He gave a tight smile. This was...not planned.

She blinked, and then righted the tray before setting it on the buffet table. "I didn't realize you were a guest." Her eyes were so wide he could see the whites all around them.

He nodded. "I didn't realize you were staying here, too." Didn't think that one through, had he?

Complicated, he thought, and not exactly an

unwelcome scenario, other than the fact that he wasn't here for fun.

And he should have remembered that last night. Should have never left his room, really. Instead, he'd gone looking for distraction. And found it.

She laughed softly. "Oh, I'm not a guest. I'm the owner."

Now it was his turn to be shocked. "You own this place?"

She nodded and gave a boastful smile. "The Harper House Inn. I'm Bridget Harper."

And I'm in trouble, Jack thought.

"Jack." He gave an uneasy smile as he replayed last night. It hadn't been a dream. He'd most definitely kissed this woman. A woman he wasn't supposed to see again. Certainly not a mere matter of hours later.

"Well, Jack, please help yourself to some pastries and coffee." She didn't make eye contact as she gestured to the spread. "If there's anything you need, I'm around. Check out is at noon."

Was it him, or did her voice take on a disappointed edge on that last line?

"Oh, I'm not checking out," he said, clearing his throat. At least he hadn't planned to. Now he wondered if he should pack his bags, head back to the city. But then he thought of his book. And the deadline. And the threatening calls from his agent. And the fact that after searching online this was the only inn he'd found with two weeks of availability.

"Oh." Bridget looked startled. "Are you extending the stay by another night?"

"I'm here for two weeks, actually."

Bridget paused. "Room Four?"

He glanced at her, sensing there was underlying meaning in her question. "That's right. Room Four."

She sucked in a breath and began backing out of the room, her eyes fixed on the buffet table. "Well. I'll just…let you…enjoy your breakfast," she finished with a smile, before turning and disappearing into the kitchen.

Jack stood with a plate in his hand, weighing his options, and not the pastry variety.

He could pack his bags, be home in a few hours. Or he could bunker down and get to work here as planned.

He had less than fourteen days to do what he had come to do: crank out as many words as possible. Shut out the real world. Push through. Half a manuscript was due by the fifteenth of May, and despite knowing this for the better part of a year, he'd waited until today to start the damn thing.

He didn't have time to drive back to New York right now. As much as he would love to.

*

Bridget stood in the pantry, which was really a fancy word for an oversized closet, wondering just how long she could stay in there until she was needed outside. An hour? A day? Two weeks, maybe?

A tapping at the door made her jump. With a thumping heart, she reached for the handle, letting out a long sigh of relief when she saw it was just Margo.

"What's going on?" Bridget whispered.

"Why are you hiding in here?" Margo whispered back.

"I'm not." Bridget pretended to take great interest in a box of oatmeal.

"Then why are we whispering?" Margo asked.

Bridget pinched her lips and pulled her sister into the pantry, closing the door tightly behind her.

"I kissed that guy."

Margo's eyes went round. "You kissed a guy?"

As if it were such a foreign concept. Still, Bridget thought begrudgingly, her dry spell *had* lasted eight years. She hadn't even known she could kiss anymore. Turned out, it really was like riding a bike...

"That guy. I kissed *that* guy." Bridget felt like she could cry when she thought about all this implied. She'd have to face him again. Put on her innkeeper hat and offer him service, like a newspaper or suggestions for dinners in town. The thought of it was simply unbearable.

Or she could apologize. Blame it on the drink. But then, he'd known she hadn't had anything all night, hadn't he? And she'd only had a sip of champagne before he...

Her eyelids fluttered when she thought of that kiss.

Nope, she told herself, righting herself firmly. Not going there.

"Which guy?" Margo's eyes were so wide, Bridget

wasn't sure she would ever blink again.

"Room Four!" Bridget hissed in despair. "Room Four!" Of all the rooms!

"Room Four?" Margo cried. Then she burst out into laughter. "Room Four! You kissed Room Four!"

"Shh! Well, I didn't know it was Room Four when I kissed him. Obviously." Bridget set her jaw, working out this dilemma. She prided herself on professionalism. Clean bedding, fresh towels, impeccable service. And now she had gone and kissed one of her guests.

She felt a headache coming on.

"Where is he? I need a look at this guy."

"He's getting breakfast. Dark hair. Tall." *Terribly handsome*, she finished to herself.

Margo's lips curved into a mischievous smile as she set her hand on the doorknob. "I'll be back."

"Mar—" Bridget started, but it was no use. Her sister was gone, off to do her spying, while Bridget…rearranged the bottom shelf of the pantry.

In less than a minute, Margo was back.

"Well?"

"He recognized me from checking him in. Can't say I could do the same. How on earth did I miss that? He's cute!" Margo's eyes lit up.

Of course he was cute. Really cute. And cute, single men of the right age didn't frequently pass through Oyster Bay, Maine, and certainly not her inn. Harper House was more of a romantic getaway type of place, not a bachelor hangout.

Margo winced. "But he's also a pain in the ass, isn't he?"

Was he? Bridget couldn't even think about that nonsense right now. She had more pressing concerns to deal with. Like the fact that she'd kissed him, and he was staying here for two weeks.

"Are any other guests staying on?" She couldn't even remember her own reservations. What was happening to her?

"The brother and sister-in-law of the bride are staying until the morning. After that...You'd have to check." Margo gave a dramatic bite on the tip of her thumb, but Bridget could see plain as day that her sister was clearly enjoying her dilemma.

"I don't suppose there's any chance you'd be willing to stay here with me for a while?" Bridget knew it was pointless to ask, but it was worth a shot.

"Sorry, but Eddie and I have dinner plans tonight," Margo replied. "You could always try Abby."

Abby. She'd fled pretty quickly, hadn't she? Bridget thought of the conversation she'd just had with Abby and groaned. She had the unnerving sensation that she'd agreed to something with her sister that she didn't exactly intend to.

Well, she would deal with that later.

"I actually think this is a good thing," Margo had the nerve to say.

Bridget gaped at her. "Margo. I kissed a *guest*. A paying

guest. A client."

Margo tilted her head, and gave Bridget a long look. "Did you kiss him, or did he kiss you?"

Bridget blinked, trying to pull up the very memory she was so eager to banish just a short while ago. There had been drinks and conversation and then..."He kissed me."

And had he. It wasn't a short, eager, sloppy kiss. It wasn't wild or desperate either. It was just slow and nice and...Oh, God. Did she just shiver?

Right. Rearranging the pantry. For the next two weeks.

"Well, then you've done nothing wrong! And really, Bridget, wasn't it about time that you got back out there? I mean, God knows Ryan has moved on."

"Nice." Bridget frowned at the mention of her ex, whose girlfriends rotated with the cycles of the moon, it would seem.

"I'm just saying that Emma is older now. You're settled. You've been on your own long enough. Wouldn't it be nice to have a man in your life again?"

Bridget had never dared to give that much thought. She'd been too busy raising Emma, and then taking care of Mimi, and lately, making a go of this place.

"I'm fine on my own," she said firmly.

"Yes, but are you happy?"

"I've never been happier! We kept this house. I finally got Emma out of that apartment we'd been living in since the divorce. And I have my own business."

"And what do you do for fun?" Margo crossed her arms and leaned against the wall, patiently waiting for an answer.

Bridget racked her mind for an answer. Fun? She didn't do fun. Fun was sometimes shopping with Emma, or curling up together on the couch in her bedroom, where they'd watch a movie. She sometimes met her sisters for coffee, but that was a bit rare. She used to go to dinner at Trish and Jeffrey's house, once a month, but lately, she'd struggled to break away from the inn, even to visit her oldest and dearest friends...

"If you must know, I had every intention of taking my latest J.R. Anderson book down to the beach today and reading for an hour before Ryan dropped Emma off." She jutted her chin. There.

Margo sputtered into laughter. "Sitting by yourself and reading is relaxing, not fun. You're still young, Bridget. And successful. And clearly Room Four finds you attractive."

Oh, Bridget wished that thought didn't fill her with such excitement.

"I'm just saying, there are a lot worse things in life than a handsome man under your roof for the next two weeks," Margo pointed out.

Bridget considered this thought for a moment as she slid the oatmeal back onto its place on the shelf. Two weeks with a handsome man under her roof. She gave a little smile. No harm in that at all.

Chapter Four

For the first time in possibly her entire existence, Abby woke without the assistance of an alarm, the phone ringing, or a less than happy parent flickering the lights and pulling the curtains open, like her mom used to do when it was time for school.

She showered and dressed, even before she'd had her morning cup of coffee—also a first—and, opting for instant brew to save time, sat down at her small dining table with the mug.

The notebook she'd been writing in on Saturday was still open to her pathetic list of job prospects, and with a satisfied grin, she ripped off the page and wadded it into a ball. She wouldn't be needing that anymore!

With any luck, she wouldn't ever have to job search again. Sure, it was just breakfast duties for now, but if things worked out, Bridget might increase her responsibilities—offer up dinner once in a while, or afternoon tea!

Yes, high tea! She wrote that down at the top of her list and underlined it three times so she would remember to bring it up with Bridget next time they met. Abby made delicious scones, not the dry variety that Angie's carried. Oh, sure, Angie excelled at muffins and the occasional Bundt cake, but soon the Harper House guests would be treated to better fare. All the grandpas at Serenity Hills raved about her blueberry scones. She'd make plain ones, too, and serve them with clotted cream and lemon curd and...

She was getting ahead of herself. What she needed to do now was come up with a weekly menu, and then a shopping list. Bridget hadn't given her an official start date, but those were trivial details that could be discussed later. Clearly, she had her hands full with a packed house at the moment. She'd check in on her later today, or tomorrow. Nail down the plan.

With a racing heart, Abby stood and crossed the room to her bookcase, which was stacked high with dog-eared cooking magazines and a few recipe books she splurged on when she couldn't resist. There were so many recipes she'd been eager to try!

But that was no matter now. She'd hand the receipt over to Bridget, who would reimburse her.

And as for not having anyone to cook or bake for,

well, she had always brought treats for the folks at Serenity Hills when she visited Mimi, which was sometimes two or three times a week. Deb at the front desk just adored her chocolate chip cookies, and Ron in the cafeteria had offered her a job more than once (but the whole hairnet thing really didn't appeal to her anymore than the dentures some of the residents left sitting on the table, next to their pudding). Mimi couldn't get enough of her baked mac and cheese, and requested it at least once a month, to which Abby was of course happy to oblige.

Mimi always encouraged her culinary efforts. It was a pastime they'd shared together, after all, in the big bright kitchen at what was now the inn, right up until a year ago when she'd moved into the home. Sometimes Mimi encouraged her to apply for a job at her Uncle Chip's restaurant, but The Lantern was a tried and true establishment; their menu hadn't budged since she was a toddler. That was hardly inspiring.

The only people Abby hadn't shared her hobby with were her sisters. Until this weekend, that was, when Bridget had forced her hand.

Well, now they'd seen. Maybe they'd finally stop seeing her as their baby sister and more of their equal.

Abby gathered up a stack of her favorite back issues and books and carried them back to the table. By the time she thought to reach for her mug for her first sip of coffee, it had grown cold, but she'd somehow never felt more energized.

She'd treat herself to a coffee at Angie's Café (one thing, with certainty, that Angie got right). And then...Then she'd get to work.

The thought of that had certainly never felt sweeter.

*

Usually after Bridget dropped Emma off at school, she went home to clean the kitchen from the breakfast dishes, and make the guest room rounds—making beds and changing sheets and hanging fresh towels from the hooks in the bathroom. Other days she stopped in town first. There were always groceries to buy or staples to replenish, like the lavender soap that was only carried at The Apothecary, a delightfully eclectic shop that carried everything from silk scarves to costume jewelry to imported soap.

She didn't need to run errands today, but that didn't mean she would be hurrying back to the inn either. The last of the wedding guests had checked out first thing this morning, and with the next round of guests not scheduled to arrive until tomorrow afternoon, that meant the only person in the house was Jack.

Not that she'd have to worry about that, per se. Jack hadn't emerged from his room, that she was aware of, since yesterday morning, when she'd had the shock of her life. When she'd gone upstairs a while later to strip the beds, the DO NOT DISTURB sign was hanging from the brass doorknob, just as it was again this morning when she'd helped her other two guests carry their luggage out to their car. The television was off, and the shower wasn't running. Room Four was completely silent.

Perhaps Jack liked to sleep in. But then, that didn't explain why he'd stayed in there all day yesterday, when she'd gone upstairs to restock the linen closet with fresh towels.

Did the man not eat? Was he dead?

Eventually she'd have to check on him.

She sighed. But not now.

Books by the Bay was just ahead on the corner and Bridget hurried to the door, knowing that she'd probably be the first customer of the day and rather hoping she was. Her oldest friend, Trish McDowell, had taken over the shop three years ago, when her youngest started kindergarten, and when old Horace Lawson decided he'd had enough of the dusty secondhand store he was running back then. Trish came in and transformed the place, with more than just a fresh coat of paint. She sold off the inventory at a bargain, and what didn't sell she donated to charity. She then turned the storefront into a proper bookstore, with cozy armchairs and story hour and tables and shelves arranged by topic, whereas poor Horace's system was to just stack as many books as he could, any which way, and let everyone browse until they grew frustrated.

The bell above the door chimed when she pushed through, and Bridget craned her neck for her friend as she wandered around the front table to her favorite section.

"Don't tell me you're here for another one already," Trish remarked jokingly as she came up from behind the counter.

"What can I say?" Bridget shrugged. "They're my guilty pleasure."

Trish just shook her head and motioned to the New Release table, where sure enough, the latest J.R. Anderson novel was on full display.

"Don't you get tired of all those happy endings?" Trish asked, as Bridget eagerly picked up the paperback and studied its cover.

"I happen to like happy endings," Bridget said, as she turned over the back to scan the blurb. "But maybe that's because I'm still searching for one myself."

Trish gave a sympathetic smile. "Have you considered dipping your toe in the dating pool again?" There was hope in her voice that Bridget secretly resented, even though she knew her friend was just being helpful. For years, Trish and her husband, Jeffrey, had been inviting Bridget over on the nights that Ryan had Emma, always with an ulterior motive. Their matchmaking ranged from the man who spent an hour showing everyone pictures of his cat, to the man who clearly just wanted a maid for his three rowdy and motherless boys, to the man who still lived at home and was looking for a woman to do everything his mother currently did for him.

"No," Bridget lied, keeping her gaze firmly on the

cover of her favorite author's newest release. After all, less than forty-eight hours ago, she had dared to think of dating again, dating a certain tall, dark, and handsome stranger who had kissed the surprise right off her lips. It was like something straight out of her favorite series. A romantic, and completely unexpected, moment. It was perfect, really. Perfect enough to let her lie awake imagining it could happen again.

She set the book firmly on the counter and removed her wallet. "After all, who needs a man when I have J.R. Anderson?"

Trish shook her head, but she was smiling nonetheless as she rang up the order and dropped the book into a brown paper bag.

"Whoever this J.R. woman is, she's clearly a success."

"Tell me about it," Bridget said. She'd devoured the first series in record time, and she doubted this book would last through the week. But then, it was the perfect distraction. Just what she needed, to engross herself in a fantasy and forget about the real one right upstairs from her bedroom...

"How did the Carrington wedding go, by the way?" Trish picked up a stack of books and motioned for Bridget to follow her. Deciding to make herself useful, Bridget picked up another stack and wandered over to the children's corner, where she set the picture books on a table.

"It was good," she said, frowning.

"You don't sound very convinced," Trish remarked.

"Oh, it's just that…" Bridget paused. There was nothing keeping her from admitting that she'd had a romantic interaction (was that what it was?) with a guest. Trish would no doubt be thrilled and want all the details over a cup of tea. It was tempting…except for the fact that admitting it to Trish meant prolonging the memory, and the hope that had come with it. No, best to just forget it. After all, it wasn't like it had happened again. Or would happen again…"Well, the caterers were late."

"Oh no!" Trish pulled a face as she wedged a hardback onto the shelf. "And Dennis Carrington is a hard man to please!"

"Exactly," Bridget said, thinking of how close she'd come to a terrible write-up on the front page of the paper.

"How'd you fix that?"

Bridget picked the first book off the stack and skimmed the back. "I had Abby come over to help."

"Abby?" Trish turned to her in surprise.

"I know," Bridget replied, as she set the book down. "But she really stepped up. I was impressed." Not impressed enough to offer her sister a job, but that was a discussion she'd need to have later. Right now, she had more pressing matters at hand. Like figuring out how to avoid going home for the next two weeks. She picked up the book again, and, finding its spot on the shelf, slid it into place.

The bells on the door chimed in the distance behind

them, and Trish looked up to greet the customer. "Welcome to Books by the Bay," she said. "Can I help you with anything?"

"Just browsing," Bridget heard a man reply.

Her hands froze as she was sliding another book onto the shelf. It wasn't just any man's voice. It was the voice she had replayed over and over and over again.

Panicked, she turned to see Jack himself, standing at the front table, surveying the newest releases. She closed her eyes and turned back to Trish, wondering if her friend would allow her exit out of the back storage room.

Instead, Trish mouthed, "Cute!"

Of course. Trish the matchmaker. She only had one thing on her mind.

"I already know him," Bridget informed her in a low whisper.

Trish's eyes widened. "Do tell!"

"It's not like that," Bridget said. Actually, it sort of was like that. For a moment. "He's a guest at the inn."

"Oh? But you're usually more friendly and outgoing with guests." Trish paused, as a knowing smile took over her mouth. "Oh, I see."

Bridget chanced a glance toward the front of the store, but Jack was mercifully engrossed in a book, his back slightly to the children's corner, which he would no doubt avoid. A man who didn't believe in marriage probably had no interest in kids, either.

Bridget eyed the playhouse and did some mental calculations. She might just fit in there, if she rolled herself into a ball.

"So, a handsome, seemingly single man is staying at your inn…And you fail to mention this to me?" Trish pinched her lips in disapproval.

"There's nothing to tell," Bridget remarked. But, oh, there was so much to tell! "He's a guest. He seems to like to keep to himself. I'm giving him some privacy."

"If you say so," Trish said pertly.

Bridget rolled her eyes, annoyed that her friend knew her so well that she wasn't going to believe any of her excuses. Of course, under normal circumstances she would go over, greet her guest, and offer up some other suggestions of places to visit while in town.

And she didn't want to be rude. Or unprofessional.

Maybe she'd just say hello…

"I'll say hello to him on my way out," she informed Trish, whose mouth seemed to twitch.

"You do that. Good plan." Trish winked.

Oh, for God's sake.

Bridget looked at her watch. Well, there was no use hiding out in the store all morning, not when the person she was running from was now less than ten feet away. She still had to strip the bedding from the rooms that had just been vacated, do the laundry, and remember to call the dance studio about Emma's recital outfit, which was at least one size too big thanks to a measuring mix-up.

Right. She'd just walk past, smile, say hello, and pretend he was a normal guest. Not a super handsome one that had taken it upon himself to kiss her the other night.

"I'm gonna go." She blew out a breath, working up the courage.

"Okay." Trish stood patiently, studying her.

Bridget bit her lower lip. "Yep. I'm going." She nodded. She could do this.

"You do that." Trish's smile was positively gloating by now.

Exasperated, Bridget snatched her bag from the table where she'd set it and began to march quickly to the door. Oh, to just sail past! She could be on the street in ten seconds if she wanted to…But no. That inn was her livelihood, and her home. And she was its representative. It was bad enough she had kissed this guest. She couldn't give him bad service, too.

"Mr. Riley!" Damn. Her voice was an octave higher than normal. From the corner of her eye, she could see Trish watching it all like a bad movie, her eyes almost as wide as her smile.

Jack looked up from the book he was holding and turned, his expression lifting in surprise when he saw her. "We meet again."

"We seem to have a way of doing that." There. This wasn't so bad. "It's a small town."

"So I've noticed," he said, rather grimly.

"You're from Manhattan, right?" So, okay, she had scoured over his reservation details last night.

"Correct." He set down the book he'd been looking

through. A murder mystery, she noted.

"Can't say we have as much excitement in Oyster Bay as the big city, but there's plenty to do. I'm happy to point out some—"

He was shaking his head. "I have to get back to work soon. I just came in to browse for a bit. Clear my head."

She knew a hint when she saw one. "Well, I won't disturb you then," she said with a tight smile.

She turned to go, but he stopped her. "I could use some good dinner recommendations."

She could feel Trish watching her, and from her periphery sensed an eager nodding from her friend. Keep it going, she could imagine her saying. You can do this!

"Oh. Okay." She tried to think of the names of the various restaurants in town, but for some reason, her entire mind had gone blank. "There's...The Lantern."

For God's sake, her own uncle's restaurant, and she hadn't thought of it!

"Dunley's has pub food," she said, naming her ex-husband's establishment out of sheer desperation. Now she could sense Trish shaking her head in total disappointment. "Nice bar scene." If he was into that type of thing...Like picking up random women for a bit of fun. Or...a kiss?

He shook his head. "I prefer something quieter. Does the inn offer anything?"

No, it did not, but Bridget hated to turn down a guest's request. And he was her only guest at the moment…

"You're welcome to join me and my daughter for dinner tonight."

She could practically hear Trish gasp across the room. She kept her eyes trained on Jack. On his gleaming blue eyes and that five o'clock shadow on that square jaw. Her heart began to pound while she waited for his response.

"I didn't realize you had a daughter," he said, the pinch between his brow unreadable.

"I'm one of the statistics you mentioned the other night," she said, with a little smile. It felt strange to mention the night of the wedding, but there was no use skirting their first meeting. "Does six thirty work for you? I'm making lasagna. House specialty."

"She does make a mean lasagna!" Trish called out, and Bridget flashed her with a warning look.

He hesitated, but only for a moment. "Lasagna happens to be my favorite comfort food. Six thirty it is."

Six thirty it was then. A date. Or at least…dinner.

She turned to go, leaving him to peruse the bookstore, and she wasn't even to the corner before her phone pinged with a text from Trish. She smiled without even having to read it.

Life hadn't been this exciting in…a long time.

Chapter Five

Jack didn't see a choice. He sat down at his computer, pulled up a blank page, and started his story. In a bookstore. There, that trip into town hadn't been a complete waste of time. Still, he couldn't spend his days wandering the shops if he expected to be productive.

He set his egg timer for an hour, vowing not to stop typing until the alarm went off, even though he knew this was a cheap trick. Over the years, he'd played a variety of games like this, tactics designed to motivate himself, but he couldn't outsmart his own mind. And for the life of himself, he couldn't stay focused either.

Once he could sit at his desk for hours, from afternoon until evening, sometimes not even realizing that the room had grown dark. Erin would come in, bringing him cups of coffee, and later, a glass of wine, her subtle way of telling him it was time to stop for the day and come pay her a little attention.

But he hadn't paid her attention, had he? Instead, he'd pointed out his deadline, the words that needed to be written, the work that needed to be done.

He closed his eyes at the memory. Well. No use thinking about that now.

What was done was done. And it wouldn't be repeated.

He stared at the screen, his fingers hunched over the keyboard, motionless. The egg timer was doing its thing, but he still wasn't doing his. Where was he? Oh, yes, a bookstore. A small bookstore in a small town. His readers liked small towns. So did his editor. And right now, that was all that mattered.

He'd get the words down, tell a story that readers wanted to read, and then…Then he didn't know. The world felt open, but it didn't feel full of possibility, not anymore. He had money to live on for a while, and there were times when he'd considered transitioning his skills into something else, like journalism, or even editing, but he hadn't given into that daydream in a while. Dreams were for those who believed they might actually come true.

A daydreamer, he thought, jotting that thought down in the notebook he always kept next to his keyboard, but which was frequently blank these days. A daydreamer in a bookstore in a small, Maine town.

It would have to do.

Somehow, he managed to write until the egg timer

went off. He looked down at his word count, at the bit of work he'd chipped off of what sometimes felt like an overwhelming task. He'd written nine hundred eighty-two words.

He didn't want to calculate how many more words were left to go.

Still, it was a start, and that was something. He didn't have another hour-long sprint in him, and soon it would be time for dinner anyway. Maybe he'd go down early, read in the lobby near one of those big fireplaces.

He jotted something down in his notebook. Perhaps he'd set the bulk of the story in an old house, like this one. Yes, yes, that was an idea he could work with.

With that in mind, he went off to explore.

Oh, who was he kidding? He was going downstairs, to the lobby, and no amount of telling himself otherwise could make up for the undeniable fact that he was hoping to see Bridget again.

*

Bridget set the oven to three seventy-five and looked over at Emma, who was in charge of sprinkling the cheese over the top of the lasagna—a job she took quite seriously, if the pinched expression on her face said anything.

"That's perfect," Bridget said, swooping the dish away before Emma could empty the rest of the bag over the top. "Why don't you go finish your homework while I get dinner ready?"

"We don't usually have guests for dinner," Emma said suspiciously as she stepped away from the counter and walked over to the kitchen table.

"Of course we do! Sometimes Margo and Abby come over."

"No, a *guest*." Emma opened her unicorn pencil case and took out a sparkly pink pencil.

Bridget didn't know whether to feel proud or sad at how astute her daughter was becoming. Sometimes, she couldn't help but miss the days when Emma still played with building blocks and loved nothing more than to crawl into her lap. Back then she still believed that broccoli were little trees. Now, Bridget couldn't pull anything past her.

"Well, we only have one guest today, so it's the hospitable thing to do." Yes, that's all it was.

Still, she'd put on her best pair of jeans and her newish top, the one Margo had insisted she buy on rare a shopping trip last month.

She reached up and touched her hair. Usually she wore it up during the day—it was easier to keep it off her face when she was running around—but tonight she'd left it down, and now she felt self-conscious, wondering if it appeared like she was trying too hard.

She eyed the bottle of wine she'd set on the center island. Too much?

The stairs creaked—a sound that was usually drowned out by other noise in the house—but tonight, it was crystal clear. Bridget felt herself pale. My God, he was coming down. Early! Quickly, she shoved the lasagna into the oven.

"Emma, stay right here," she said, her eyes darting from the doorway to the dining room to the doorway to her living quarters, wondering which choice was a better bet.

Too late. There he was, in jeans and a rugby shirt and, God help her, a five o'clock shadow. Did the man never shave? He gave her a lazy smile and shame on her if her stomach didn't roll over.

Immediately his eyes went to the table, and he gave a puzzled look at Emma before giving a small smile. "Hello," he said.

"Are you the guest who is having dinner with us tonight?" Emma asked, pencil still poised over her math sheet.

"If I'm still invited," he said, cocking an eyebrow in Bridget's direction.

"Mom took out a bottle of wine, just for you," Emma informed him.

Bridget felt her back teeth graze against her smile. No explaining that one away. Still. She'd try.

"Mr. Riley is our guest, Emma," she said pointedly. To Jack she said, "Can I offer you a glass of wine?"

"Actually, that would be great," he said, much to her relief.

Grateful for a reason to keep busy, she walked around

to a drawer and pulled out the corkscrew.

"I'm afraid the lasagna still has a ways to go," she said.

"I don't mind waiting," he said with a friendly grin. "I needed a break."

A break? What was it he was doing up there in that room all day? "Keeping busy?" She popped the cork free and poured two glasses of Cabernet.

"I'm trying," he said, a little sheepishly. "I came here to get some work done."

Ah, well that explained things. Sort of. He wanted peace and quiet. No wonder he was complaining about all the noise from the wedding. "What is it that you do?"

She was only making conversation, but she was surprised when he replied, "I'm a writer."

"A writer?" She blinked.

"That surprise you?" He took the glass from her hand and took a sip.

"A little," she admitted. "I might have pinned you for a businessman."

At this, he laughed. "No, definitely not."

"So a creative type then." She couldn't help but be a little pleased. She glanced at the timer. They still had quite a bit of time until dinner. "We could go onto the back porch, or into the lobby, if you'd like."

"The porch," he said, nodding. "I could use the fresh air."

Bridget took her wine glass and gave Emma one last glance to make sure homework was actually being done. Then she led Jack into the hallway and out the back

French doors of what used to be the sunroom and now had turned into a second lobby—a conservatory of sorts, with walls of windows that lent a view of the ocean.

The temperature had dropped since she'd come back from picking Emma up at school, and a salty breeze blew off the water.

Jack hovered near the doorway, one hand thrust in his pocket, the other clutching his wine glass. The sea rolled in behind him, but Bridget wasn't admiring the view for once.

"I owe you an apology," he said, glancing up at her. "For the other night. It was...out of character."

Bridget felt her face heat and wished that she wasn't standing a mere two feet from him, with no way to create distance but to back up straight against the exterior wall of the house. "It was a party..." She gave an uneasy smile, wishing that he hadn't brought up the kiss almost as much as she was relieved he had.

"Anyway," he said, stiffening. "I can assure you that it won't happen again."

Bridget felt the air deflate from her as fast as a popped balloon. "Well. Thank you for making that clear."

Jack's eyes widened. "Oh. Please don't...It's not that I don't find you attractive."

Now it was Jack's turn to blush. Bridget couldn't help but smile. At the compliment. And at how awkward this seemed to make him.

"It's that..."

She held up a hand, deciding to let him off the hook. "You don't believe in romance. I get it."

"No. I mean…No, I guess I don't believe in it, no."

There was a time, she had to admit, that she hadn't believed in it either. Still, hearing those words spoken aloud…it should be all she needed to hear. The man was a guest. He was only passing through town. And he didn't believe in love.

Seriously, Bridget, the facts are on the table. How was this any different than all the red flags Ryan was waving before she eloped with him? The dates he'd stand her up on, the endless talk about his career and not about family.

Bridget dropped onto one of the rocking chairs, and Jack did the same.

"So, despite this sentiment, do you make a habit of crashing weddings?"

He grinned, a bashful, boyish grin that had to go and make her feel all soft and swoony despite her misgivings. "No. And I didn't realize I'd be caught, either."

"I suppose the party was a bit loud, if you were trying to work…"

"Maddening," he said, his eyes gleaming. "What choice did I have but to come down and see what all the fuss was about?"

"I think you're forgiven. Weddings *can* be a fun time," she said with a small smile.

"They can," he said, and the faraway look that took over his expression made her wonder, for one, fleeting moment, if all his protestations about love and romance were just an excuse.

Nonsense. What did it matter? He'd made his thoughts clear. He was a nice man, who had kissed her, and who clearly didn't plan on taking it any further.

"So," she said, wanting to get back to the topic they'd reached in the kitchen. A safe subject, surely. "What do you write?"

"Fiction," he said. Then, after a pause, "Fantasy."

"Novels?" Well, this just got better and better. She'd been expecting him to say that he wrote for a newspaper or magazine.

He nodded. "But after this one, I'm taking a break. Maybe I'll travel for a bit. I haven't really thought that far ahead."

"That sounds nice." Bridget leaned her head back wistfully.

"Traveling?"

"And not thinking ahead." She grinned. "I'm a planner. Always have been."

His mouth seemed to thin. "The problem with planning is that life rarely goes to plan."

"My, you're cynical!" she exclaimed. And she was a fool for doubting his declarations, for wanting him to be someone he clearly wasn't.

That kind of thinking only led to trouble.

He just shrugged. "But I'm right, aren't I?"

She had to admit that yes, he was. After all, where had all her grand plans taken her? She'd never imagined she'd be divorced, a single mom with a baby under the age of one. She'd never imagined a life without more children, either. No siblings for Emma.

But then, she'd never even dared to imagine that she might someday have the fortune of owning this house, rather than selling it to a complete stranger, either.

"Sometimes the surprises turn out okay," she said with a smile.

He grumbled something inaudible under his breath and took a long sip of his wine.

"Look at me, for example," she said. "I grew up in this house. I left it, got married, made a dozen plans for myself, most of which didn't happen, and now here I am, back where I started, but in a different role."

"You're happy." His voice was filled with wonder as he pondered the statement.

Bridget nodded. "Very much so. I love this house. A year ago, my sisters and I didn't think we'd be able to hold onto it."

"What about your parents?" he asked, and even though the question was natural, she couldn't help but look away.

"They died in a car accident. Right after Emma was born." She took a sip of her wine.

"Wow." He had the same shell-shocked reaction everyone did when they learned this. "I'm sorry."

She shrugged. "It's been a long time." But somehow, she thought to herself, it still felt like yesterday. "My grandmother was like a parent to me and my sisters for years. My middle sister and I handled it well enough, but my youngest sister, Abby…" She trailed off. Just thinking of Abby made her need another sip of wine. "Abby needed parents. Still does."

"She has you," Jack pointed out.

"Yes, but I've never been able to give her the attention she deserves. Ryan—my ex—and I split soon after my parents died, and being a single mother with an infant was, well, a challenge." She felt sad, still, thinking back on that time. It was a dark time, when life felt so bleak even though she knew that it should have been so happy. It was never how she'd imagined the first year of Emma's life to be, overshadowed by life's trials.

All the more reason to make up for it now.

"Abby comes over for dinner sometimes." It wasn't much, and she always felt guilty, thinking that she should be doing more, but Abby kept busy, and well, there wasn't any other time. Now that she was running the inn, she seemed to have less time than more, but at least she was settled.

If only Abby could do the same…

"Room Four actually used to be Abby's room," Bridget said, thinking of the way the room used to look, with purple walls and posters of celebrities all over the walls. "When I renovated the house into an inn, we obviously changed things a bit. My sister Margo helped with that. It's still home, but it's different."

"Margo." He seemed to frown on the name. "I met

her, I think. Was she at the front desk on Saturday?"

"Yes!" Bridget couldn't help but feel flattered he would remember. "You have a good memory."

"Or a sharp eye for detail," he said, but she could tell he was pleased. "So it's a family business then?"

"This? Oh, no. Margo's an interior designer, but she helped me renovate the place. And Abby…" She sucked in a breath. She still had to talk to Abby. No doubt Abby was latching onto another random idea, this time brought on by Bridget calling in a favor Saturday night. Honestly, she appreciated Abby's enthusiasm, but she'd believe in it more if it wasn't so waning. "Abby's a free spirit," she said, summarizing Abby's lifestyle.

"And this drives you crazy," he said, with a knowing smile.

Bridget started to protest, but he clearly saw through it. "How'd you guess?"

He shrugged. "I tend to have a good read on people." His jaw tensed. "Most people."

Bridget wondered just who he failed to relate to when the door opened and Emma stood there, clutching a pencil and announcing that the timer had gone off.

"Already?" Bridget could hear the disappointment in her tone. She'd been enjoying this one-on-one time, outside on the porch. Tomorrow more guests would arrive and by Friday, they'd have a full house. "Well, I suppose we should go in."

"I already washed my hands," Emma announced. "And I set the table, too."

Bridget reached for Emma's hand and gave it a squeeze. "Thank you!"

"You're busy," Emma said sagely. Looking up at Jack, who was right behind them, she said, "My mom has a lot of laundry to do. And errands. And then there's my great-grandmother to worry about, and Aunt Abby, who can't get her life together and really needs a steady job..."

Jack laughed, and Bridget shot Emma a warning look. "Remember what we talked about, Emma? What we discuss as a family, stays within the family?"

"Like what we talk about at our family dinners?"

"Exactly," Bridget said, releasing her daughter's hand as they entered the kitchen. Sure enough, the timer was beeping, and as Bridget opened the oven, she could tell that the lasagna was ready. Grabbing two oven mitts, she slid the heavy dish from the rack and set it on the stove top.

"We can start with salad while it cools," she said, noticing that Jack had already taken his place at the table.

Ryan's place, she realized with a pang. For some reason, she always kept the head chair empty, choosing instead to sit across from Emma, her sisters taking their own side chairs when they stopped by for a meal.

It was silly, she knew. After all, she and Ryan had split long before family meals had started. Their relationship was ending when Emma was barely able to sit in a highchair. But still, their places had been established. Ryan cooked—when he was home to cook and not at the restaurant—and Ryan sat at the head of the table.

And for eight long years that chair had remained empty.

Until tonight.

"Well!" Bridget cleared her throat, and before she could think any more about the way life had turned out, she lifted the salad bowl and set it on the center of the table. When she pulled back, she noticed Jack looking up at her, and a guilty flush seemed to spread over his face before he looked away.

Had he been...checking her out? She hadn't been checked out since, well, not counting Saturday night, since before Emma was born. Now in her mid-thirties, she sort of assumed that phase of life was over.

Self-consciously, she tucked herself into her own chair, lifting her wine glass to hide her smile.

"So, Mommy, how was your day?" Emma asked, and Bridget glanced over at Jack to see his brow furrow in confusion.

"Very good, Emma. How was yours?"

"Well..." Emma's eyes became round with excitement. "Mary Alice had to go to the principal even though it was her birthday!"

Jack served himself some salad, fighting off a grin.

"Oh my." Bridget exchanged a smile with Jack as he passed her the salad. "What prompted that?"

"She told Rebecca to shut up. Twice!"

Bridget turned to Jack. "Mary Alice is the third-grade troublemaker."

"So I've gathered," Jack said, his eyes gleaming.

"Was that the good part or the bad part of your day?" Bridget asked, and then realized that this too required some explanation. She turned to Jack, her heart skipping a beat when their eyes met. "We like to tell each other the good parts and the bad parts of our day, just as a way of communicating."

"I see." Jack nodded in approval. "So, Emma, which was it?"

"Oh, the best part!" Emma giggled, and Bridget couldn't help it, she started laughing at the same time as Jack.

"What was the best part of your day, Mommy?" Emma asked, and Bridget felt her pulse skip a beat.

"Right now," she said, honestly, not daring to look in Jack's direction. "You know how much I love sitting down to a family meal." It was something she'd valued so much, growing up, here in this house. Something Ryan had never prioritized, and seemingly never would. Never did.

"Must be nice to have family meals," Jack said with a sad smile.

Bridget studied him, wondering if she should ask what he meant by that, when Emma cut in, "Don't you have a wife?"

"Emma!" Bridget scolded, feeling her cheeks heat.

But Jack just laughed. "It's okay," he reassured her, before turning to Emma. "No, I do not have a wife."

"Mommy doesn't have a husband either," Emma said sagely. "Daddy has girlfriends. Mommy calls them flavors of the month."

"Emma!" Bridget closed her eyes, but the sound of Jack's laughter forced them open again. "I'm sorry," she said. "We're going through a strange phase now where you can't say anything without it coming back at you."

"Do you have any kids?" Emma asked.

Bridget had to admit, that despite Emma's rudeness, she was just as eager for the answers.

"No, but I do have a goldfish."

Emma giggled, and Bridget found herself laughing. "A goldfish?"

"That's right. Fred. Fred the fish."

"Where is he? I want to see him!" Emma said excitedly.

"Oh now, he's back at my apartment in New York. But...maybe if I visit again, I'll bring him." Jack's brow seemed to pinch as he took another bite of his food, but when he glanced up at her, his eyes were warm and so intense that Bridget had to tear herself away.

"More wine?" she asked, refilling his glass, and her own, before even waiting for an answer.

More wine, she thought, silently answering for them both. It was definitely time for more wine.

*

The last time Jack had dined with someone other than his agent was back when he and Erin were still together.

The divorce had cost him more than just their Upper West Side apartment; it had meant that friends chose sides, and most seemed to follow Erin. He wasn't surprised—Erin and the wives were friends first, and then Jack and the husbands were friends by default. Erin always used to say that when they had kids, they'd become friends with their children's friends' parents. But that day had never arrived.

"This was delicious," Jack said as he helped Bridget clear the plates.

"Please, let me!" Bridget looked momentarily panicked as she took the lasagna dish from him. "You're my guest!"

"Last I checked, dinner wasn't included in the price of the room," he reminded her, and was rewarded with a small smile. "Let me. Please. It keeps me from going back to my room and staring at my computer screen."

"If you insist." She sighed as she turned on the tap and rinsed the plates. "Writer's block?"

"Guess you could call it that," he said, though it was more than that, really. More like a life block. A dead end. He'd lost his momentum, his drive, his passion.

"I'm afraid I can't help you with that," she said. "The most I ever wrote was a twenty-page essay in college on the impact of birth order and personality."

He laughed. "Psych major?"

"Gee, how'd you guess?"

"And where'd you fall in that scenario?" He couldn't

help it, he was eager to know more. It had been a long time since he'd wanted to get to know anyone. But Bridget…she was pleasant and kind and warm.

And pretty. Very, very pretty.

"First born. Classic Type-A personality." She laughed. "How about you? Any brothers or sisters?"

"A half-sister," Jack said. "But we're fifteen years apart and she lives in California, where my dad is. I can't exactly say we're close."

"And your mother?"

"She's remarried too. No kids, though. She's down in Florida. I don't visit much."

"Well, you're an interesting cross between an only child and a first born, then." Bridget gave him a mischievous smile.

"And what does that make me?"

"Independent? I'd have to check my notes, though. It's, uh, been a while." She laughed again.

"Independent sounds about right," he said. "I suppose that's why I like New York. I can do my thing. Fade into the crowd."

"Then you'd probably have a hard time in Oyster Bay," she said, frowning a little. "In a town this small, well, let's just say that some people know things about me before I even know."

"Such as?"

"Oh, who my sister's dating. Who my ex is dating…"

He grimaced. "Ouch."

"In a way," she said. "Sometimes it's nice to be

forewarned."

"My ex is actually in the same city as me, too. Luckily for me, New York is a little bigger." He froze. He wasn't used to talking about Erin. Most days, he didn't even like thinking about her. But talking to Bridget was easy. Natural, even.

Bridget frowned. "I didn't realize you were married."

"Was," he stressed. "Never again."

Bridget nodded, and looked away, and for a reason he couldn't justify, he wished he hadn't come down so hard on the idea.

She set the plates into the dishwasher and adjusted the settings. For a moment, there was a flicker of silence, and Jack wondered if he'd overstayed his welcome, if Bridget was eager to get back to her daughter, or whatever else it was she did when she had the house to herself and wasn't at the mercy of a lingering guest.

"What do you usually do? For fun?" He wasn't sure if he was dragging out the night because he didn't want to go back to his room to work or because he didn't want to be alone. Or, possibly, because he wanted to be with her. He was always alone, and usually he preferred it that way. But tonight was different. Tonight he'd felt right at home, in this kitchen, with Bridget's soft laughter and Emma's funny comments, and the thought of going up to his room now, closing the door, and hearing nothing but silence depressed the hell out of him.

Bridget picked up the bottle of wine, and Jack could

see there was still a bit left. "Top you off?"

Jack nodded. "Only if you have a bit, too."

"There you go, encouraging me again," Bridget teased, and then her cheeks flushed as she evenly distributed the wine into both of their glasses.

It was awkward discussing the night of the wedding, for both of them, but Jack only half-regretted that kiss. It had been an indiscretion, a mistake. Something that couldn't be repeated.

But it had been nice.

His gaze lingered on her mouth as she brought the glass to it. He swallowed, hard. No. It couldn't be repeated.

"I suppose I'm encouraging my own," he admitted as he followed her into the lobby and took a seat in one of the loveseats near the window. Bridget seemed to hesitate before coming to sit next to him, not quite within reach. "I should be working right now. But...I needed a break."

"Is that why you booked a two-week stay here?"

He barked out a laugh. "Just the opposite. I couldn't think straight in Manhattan. Too much noise, too much...distraction." Too many memories was more like it. Everywhere he turned, he was reminded of a time and place that wasn't his anymore, when New York felt fresh and exciting and his career felt as full of potential as life itself. He'd fallen into a rut, a bad habit of taking long, meandering walks and then stopping for a drink or dinner at the bar, where he'd linger, and then finally go home to an empty, dark apartment, tell himself it was too late to work, and that he'd get to it tomorrow. But he'd run out of tomorrows. "My agent thought a change of scenery would do me good."

"And you chose Harper House Inn!" Bridget's smile was so genuine, Jack felt something in him shift. He didn't talk to people anymore. Somewhere in the past three years, he'd become a hermit.

"Well, I'm setting this particular story in an old house," he explained. It was true, even if the order of events were skewed. He'd started out with a blank slate, nothing more than the standard formula of boy meets girl, falls in love, lives happily ever after.

He almost snorted into his drink.

"Well, I hope you're finding inspiration then!"

Jack studied Bridget, suddenly feeling a desire in him that he hadn't felt in a long time, as if something was awakening. A desire to talk, to discuss. And maybe even a desire to write, to capture something in life that had gone unnoticed recently.

"I am finding inspiration," he said, realizing just how true that was.

Chapter Six

Mornings, Bridget found, were always the most challenging part of the day. Even before she'd taken over this house and opened the inn, it had been that way. Back then it had been the endless scramble of showering, dressing, making Emma's breakfast, cleaning up breakfast, checking over homework, and getting Emma to school before running to work at the real estate agency where she'd worked for eight years following her split from Ryan.

There was always something to cause delay: forgotten homework at the bottom of Emma's bag; a missing field trip permission slip, misplaced library books, or missing keys.

Today, it was missing socks.

"What do you mean you have no matching socks?"

Bridget added muffins to the basket of mixed pastries as quickly as her hands would allow her, even if she did only have one guest, and even if he probably wouldn't come out his room at all today, much to her chagrin. Still, service was service, and she wasn't about to let anything slip.

"I have a pink one and a grey one and purple one and a striped one. Oh! And one with hearts!" Emma called in delight from her bedroom.

Bridget popped the lid of a box of croissants and began arranging them in one of the baskets. The order was smaller than usual, and whatever didn't get eaten this morning, she'd bring over to Serenity Hills when she and Emma visited Mimi after school today.

Her phone buzzed. She glanced at the screen. Margo. She'd have to call her back.

"There are some with polka dots!" Emma offered.

Bridget bit back her frustration. She dumped the remaining pastries in the basket, flipped over the ones that landed askew, and all but ran them into the dining room, where she'd already set up the fruit and yogurt. Even though she'd expected the dining room to be empty, she couldn't help but feel a little disappointed that Jack hadn't emerged from his room yet.

Well. No time to dwell. She had a missing sock to find and a pot of coffee to make.

"Emma," she said, as she walked into their living quarters, through the small sitting area, and into her daughter's pale pink bedroom. "If I open that drawer and find a matching pair of socks, I'm not going to be happy. I still have to make the coffee and we're supposed to leave in—" She glanced at her watch. "Six minutes!"

Emma's eyes turned comically round, and Bridget fought off a smile as she opened the top drawer of the white dresser she'd pilfered from Abby's childhood bedroom. Sure enough. No matching socks.

She frowned as she rifled through them.

"I told you there weren't any!" Emma declared, folding he arms over her chest. "I don't lie."

Bridget looked down at her daughter and stoked her cheek. Its softness never failed to surprise her. "Of course not, sweetheart. Sometimes mothers are just better at finding these things…"

And sometimes not. She stared into the contents of the drawer. "How is this even possible?" And what were the odds? One of each pair, but no match at all?

"Maybe the machine ate them," Emma offered.

It seemed like a half-reasonable explanation at the moment. "Maybe," Bridget said, shaking her head. "Well, we don't have time to bother with this right now. You'll just have to wear sandals today."

The forecast had called for sunshine and blue skies and a high of seventy. Fair enough for sandals this once.

"But what about gym class? And recess!" Emma's lower lip began to quiver.

Bridget tried not to let the impatience register on her face. "Emma. It's just for today—"

"Hello!" a voice called from the kitchen. A female voice. In fact, if Bridget didn't know better, she'd say that was her sister Abby's voice.

She hurried into the kitchen, where sure enough her sister stood, laden with shopping bags.

"I'm here to make breakfast!" she announced.

Bridget blinked. She tried to think of something diplomatic to say, something that wouldn't hurt her sister's feelings but that would nip this whole scheme of Abby's in the bud. "Abby, I—"

"Mommy!" Emma came bursting into the room, clutching a fistful of socks. "I don't want to wear mismatched socks to school!"

"Why not?" Abby said cheerfully. "They still cover your feet. And it's kind of interesting. Personally, I'd choose the one with hearts and the pink striped one."

"Really?" Emma smiled, revealing two spaces where her grown-up teeth were yet to make an appearance. "Cool."

Cool. Bridget felt a little pang in her chest. Her baby was saying words like "cool." Where was the little toddler who called her backpack a "cack cack"? Next thing Bridget knew, Emma would be asking for a cell phone and wanting to color her hair.

She sighed. For now, she should just be grateful that Emma still wanted to hold her hand. That was something. Something she'd hold on to...forever, if she could.

Emma ran off to her bedroom, and Bridget turned to

her sister. "Thank you."

Abby just shrugged. "That's what aunts are for. Especially the fun ones," she added with a grin.

Bridget eyed the shopping bags uneasily. "Why don't I take Emma to school and then we can finish our conversation from the weekend?" She could offer her one weekend a month, something to start with, and something she could supervise.

She glanced at the clock. They only had four minutes now. Hurrying, she went to the coffee machine and started a pot. "Emma, don't forget your library books!"

"Too early for coffee?" a voice behind her grumbled.

Bridget felt the hair on the back of her head stand up. He'd emerged. She'd half expected not to see him at all today…even if she had made sure to swipe her lipstick on a bit earlier than usual.

"Good morning!" she said brightly, turning to face him.

Her stomach knotted at the sight. A blue rugby shirt hugged his chest in all the right places, and his hair was perfectly tousled, as if he'd just rolled out of bed.

Her lids fluttered.

"Hello…" He gave a slow smile that undid her. "I hope it's okay that I'm in here. Or is the kitchen usually not open to guests?"

"Usually not," she admitted. "But I'm always happy to make an exception for my favorite guest."

Abby turned to her with wide eyes, and Bridget felt her cheeks start to burn.

Dear God, she was flirting. And she didn't flirt. Never had. Her own mother used to elbow her ribs and tell her that she needed to try a little harder, show the guys she was interested. Instead, she'd hidden in the corner at school dances and in the cafeteria, clinging to her friends and blushing anytime a guy looked her way.

The shy girl thing had worked with Ryan. He liked the chase. But if an eight-year dry spell said anything, it didn't work in general.

Oh, Mom, she thought, feeling that ache in her chest. What she wouldn't give for just one more conversation. One more family meal. There had been so many times over the years she still wished she could pick up the phone…especially all those long, lonely nights when Emma was a baby, and she was so overwhelmed and didn't know who to turn to for help.

"Favorite guest, or only guest?" Jack shot back, cocking an eyebrow devilishly.

"Only guest," Bridget admitted with a laugh. "Though another couple is arriving today. We'll be full up by Friday for the Flower Fest this weekend."

It was one of her favorite festivals that Oyster Bay offered, and Emma was especially looking forward to entering the hat decorating contest, even if she would be attending the event with her father this year.

"Flower Fest?" Jack didn't look sold on the idea.

Bridget started the coffee and explained, "It's an annual event to celebrate spring, really. There are flowers, of course, but…other festivities, too."

"Maybe I'll check it out," Jack said to her surprise.

She hoped the expression on her face didn't reveal how pleased she was.

"The coffee will be ready in two minutes," she said. "And while you wait, there are some pastries and fruit in the dining room."

"Same as yesterday?" he said good-naturedly.

Bridget frowned. She wasn't used to having guests stay for more than a night, two at most. "Well, yes——"

"Unless, you'd prefer an omelet?" Abby cut in, refusing to meet Bridget's eye.

Jack looked pleased. "An omelet sounds great, actually."

"Great. Spinach and goat cheese is today's special."

"Wow, that sounds delicious," Jack said, grinning, as he wandered into the dining room.

Indeed it did, Bridget thought, her lips thinning. It wasn't until he was out of ear shot that she turned to her sister, hissing, "Abby, I told you——"

"You're going to be late to school," Abby said pleasantly. "And like you said, we can talk about all this when you get back."

Oh, they would, Bridget thought, grabbing a light jacket and her car keys. They most certainly would.

*

When Jack returned to the kitchen for a cup of coffee, he had the uneasy sensation that the auburn-haired woman was giving him the once-over. He shoved his hands into the pockets of his jeans and gave her a grin, hoping it passed for friendly and not suggestive.

"I don't think we've met," she said, thrusting out a hand. "I'm Abby Harper, Bridget's younger sister."

Ah, so this was Abby. His grin came a little easier now. He almost felt like he had an advantage in this situation. "Bridget mentioned you."

"Oh?" Abby looked decidedly interested, and she showed no signs of making his omelet until he continued.

"We were talking about this house last night at dinner," he said. "She mentioned Room Four technically used to be your childhood bedroom."

"Did you say dinner?" Abby frowned. "I didn't realize Bridget was serving her guests dinner." She stepped back, seeming flustered.

Immediately, Jack realized he had stepped into something he didn't want to be a part of—a family matter that was none of his business. Abby's brow was pinched and her eyes were darting over the room. "Oh, no. It was...Well, I was hungry. And she was making a lasagna, so..." He shrugged. No use in explaining further. It was dinner. Nothing more.

Then why did it feel like something he needed to hide?

"I see." Abby's face relaxed just in time for her the corners of her mouth to curl. "Yes, I *see*."

Oh, brother. Now she was really getting the wrong impression. Jack held up a hand. "It's not what you think.

I'm…"

"Married?" Her brow lifted.

He almost laughed out loud at her audacity, but he couldn't help but like her for it. Her green eyes held his, clearly waiting for an answer.

"No," he replied.

"Engaged?"

"No. Happily single. And…very busy." He gave her a pointed look, then made a show of looking at the carton of eggs. His stomach rumbled and, much as he was enjoying Abby's company, the familiar sensation of anxiety was starting to take over, just like it did every time he thought of his looming deadline.

"Of course! The omelet. Coming right up, sir."

"I'll wait in the lobby," he said, thinking how formal and uncomfortable it would be to sit at the long dining table all by himself and be served by this woman. "Is the inn usually this quiet?"

Not that he minded. In fact, he preferred it to the drunken cheers of celebration he'd suffered through during the weekend. Still, he couldn't use it as an excuse for his lack of productivity, much as he wished.

"It always fills up by the weekends. Especially this weekend," Abby said chattily.

Jack hovered in the doorway, realizing by posing the question he wasn't going to get out of the room anytime soon.

"Flower Fest is one of the best festivals in Oyster Bay. Everyone comes out to the town green, and they fill the stands with food and flowers, and there's a live band. Crafts for the kids. Of course, when the weather is bad, they have to cancel, and just hold a giant flower sale instead at the town hall," she chattered as she finally fetched a bowl and cracked an egg into it. "But everyone comes out for it. You should go!" She looked up at him, grinning.

"I have a lot of work to do," he said, the anxiety really burning now.

"Suit yourself, but it's a lot of fun. Anyway, the inn will be full up. Couples, no doubt, in search of a romantic weekend excursion." She gave him a lingering look as he backed out of the room, finding relief in the empty shadows of the front parlor.

Still, he chuckled to himself as he sat down in an armchair near the fireplace. She was an interesting character. And he could use one of those about now.

*

Bridget pulled Emma up to the Kiss N' Cry, eager to get back to the inn, and not because of Jack. No, it was better that she didn't see him again. Better that she let last night's dinner fade into her memory like the kiss had. She'd just been hospitable. Nothing more. He was a guest, and she had food. Tonight she was having dinner with Mimi, so there would be no repeats. Definitely not.

"Did you remember your library books?" she asked as Emma unhooked her seat belt.

"They're in my locker," Emma said, shaking her head.

Bridget tried to listen to herself objectively. Was she a nag? Probably. But, really, what choice did she have?

"Have a great day at school, honey. When I pick you up, we're going over to visit Mimi."

Emma wrinkled her nose. "Is Pudgie going to be there?"

Bridget sighed. It had been Abby's brilliant idea to get their grandmother a cat when she moved into Serenity Hills—the one pet that was permitted. Unfortunately, the good intention had backfired, and everyone aside from Mimi had a problem with the obese feline.

"It's not Pudgie's fault he doesn't behave," Bridget told Emma. "It's Mimi's fault for spoiling him so much." My goodness, if anyone overheard, they would think Pudgie was a boy, not an animal. She grinned at her daughter, "Tell you what, I'll let you push Mimi's wheelchair when we go into the cafeteria."

Emma's eyes danced at this suggestion. Cheap thrills, Bridget thought, shaking her head as she watched Emma run onto the playground of the very school she'd attended a staggering number of years ago.

Not much had changed since then. The jungle gym and slide and swings had been upgraded, but the rest was the same, right down to the principal and the school librarian, who was a stickler about late books.

But a lot had changed, Bridget thought, as she circled onto Main Street and headed back to the inn. Back then she'd still lived in the big, Victorian house with her sisters and parents and grandmother. There had been Sunday dinners and festive holidays and summers that felt like they lasted forever. Later, in high school, there had been Ryan. Cool, handsome, and just charming enough to keep her hanging on, even when he'd stand her up for dates, and later, drag his feet on the topic of marriage. Once they'd finally gotten married, he'd dragged his feet about a house, and kids, spending all his energy on his restaurant instead.

Even though they'd only divorced eight years ago, it felt like a lifetime ago. Like she'd been a different person. Like she'd been a fool.

Well, never again. She wasn't going to be a fool again.

But she'd also never leave Oyster Bay. She loved it here. Loved its history and its memories. Even the tough ones.

And maybe, maybe she'd get married again. If she was lucky enough to know that, this time, it would last.

She managed to hit every green light and made it home in record time. But Abby's car wasn't the only one in the lot she'd carved out to the side of the house. Margo's silver SUV was right beside it, and fortunately no one else, meaning her newest guests were yet to arrive.

She pulled into her reserved spot closest to the house and, because she couldn't resist, smoothed her hair when she stepped out of the car.

Honestly!

She hurried up the front steps and into the foyer-turned-lobby of the large home. Glancing into the dining room, she was deflated to see that it was empty, and that Jack had probably returned to his room, where he would stay for a good portion of the day.

Relaxing her shoulders, she walked down the hall and into the kitchen, where Abby and Margo were standing at the island, deep in conversation.

"What did I miss?" she said as she set her handbag down on a stool.

"More like what did I miss!" Abby wagged her finger in Bridget's direction. "So you're serving dinner to guests now?"

Bridget felt her cheeks flush. Guilty as charged. "It was a one-time thing. I only have one guest and the man was hungry."

"Uh-huh. And I'm a blonde." Abby gestured to her auburn hair. "Sounds like a date to me."

"It wasn't a date." Wait, had Jack implied otherwise? Her heart sped up for a moment before she pushed the thought firmly back into place. She walked over to the counter to begin cleaning up the breakfast dishes, only to notice that someone had already cleaned them. Abby? More like Margo.

"Well, he couldn't stop praising your lasagna," Abby said. Before Bridget could perk up at this, she continued, "Of course, he was raving about the omelet I made him. Says it was just as good as anything he can find in New York."

Bridget picked up a rag and began scrubbing the

counters. She knew a twinge of jealousy when it struck. She still felt it at times when she went to her ex-husband's restaurant and saw him with whatever young, skinny thing he happened to be dating that week. Even though she knew his love life was a revolving door, it still hurt to feel like she'd been replaced.

"So you talked to him then?"

"Only briefly," Abby said. "Long enough to learn where he was from and how long he's here. I told him some things to do in town. "

"That's all?" Why did she care? And why did she ask? Now her sisters would never let her forget this. She glanced in their direction to see smug smiles on their faces. Yep, sure enough.

"He seemed far more interested in asking about the history of the inn than paying me any attention, if that's what you're after," Abby replied.

"That's not what I'm after," Bridget said irritably, but that wasn't true and Abby knew it. It was…exciting to have a handsome, single man upstairs, as a guest in her home. Even more exciting that he'd given her a romantic moment that had been missing from her life for long before she was even divorced. Ryan had never been one for impromptu gestures or flowers or flattery. His mind was always on something else, primarily his restaurant. So really, it was forgivable that she was still caught up in the fantasy of it all. And really, that's all it was. A fantasy. Because the reality was that a week from Friday, Jack would be on his way back to New York and she'd be alone in this house again.

Well, not entirely. She had Emma. Thank God for her.

"What brings you by?" she asked Margo.

Her middle sister beamed, and something in the look in her eyes gave Bridget the answer. Her stomach felt funny, and she suddenly wished she hadn't asked, or that she could feel happier in this moment than she did.

"Well, I was waiting to have you both together, and seeing as I do…" Margo held out her left hand and wiggled her fingers to reveal a beautiful diamond ring. "Eddie proposed last night!"

Bridget blinked, knowing she should react differently. She should squeal with delight, run over and fling her arms around Margo's shoulders, tell her this was the best news she'd ever heard. But, she couldn't. Instead, all she could think was that Margo had never known divorce the way Bridget knew divorce. Margo and her husband had split, amicably, and then Margo had soon thereafter reconciled with her high school sweetheart, whereas Bridget had struggled as a single mother on a fixed income without a single date (unless you called last night's lasagna dinner a date, which it wasn't) for eight years and counting.

Call her selfish, and maybe she was, but instead of feeling happy for Margo, all she felt was sorry for herself.

The ache in her chest was still pulling hard when she tore her gaze from the sparkling diamond to Margo's face, and all at once, that pity was replaced with shame.

Margo's smile hadn't been this bright in more years than Bridget could count. She'd found her happy ending, and Bridget was always a sap when it came to those.

"I'm so happy for you!" she said, feeling it, right to the heart, as she went over and hugged her sister.

"He proposed on a Monday night?" Abby was saying in a tone that implied she had opinions on this.

"He was going to wait until the Flower Fest this weekend, but well..." Margo shrugged. "We had a nice dinner, and one thing led to another."

"I think Monday is a perfect night for an engagement." Bridget gave Abby a scolding look. "It's less expected that way. More romantic."

"When do you think you'll get married?" Abby wanted to know.

"Soon," Margo replied. "Three weeks. Well, two weeks from Saturday."

"Three weeks!" Bridget couldn't hide her shock. Margo hadn't even been single yet, and now she was getting married again? She'd never known what it felt like to eat dinner alone, with only the television to keep you company, or to go to a New Year's Eve party without a date, and certainly no one to kiss you at the stroke of midnight.

"It's my second marriage, and I already did the big church wedding thing," Margo explained. "I want to get married the way I always wanted to. Here, in the backyard of this house. We already lost so much time...We didn't want to waste any more."

Now all those self-pitying thoughts officially screeched to a halt. "You want to get married *here*? In three weeks?"

Margo was nodding, but she was biting her lower lip, her eyes seeming to search Bridget's for approval. "It wouldn't have to be anything fancy. Just forty or fifty people or so."

Oh my God. Bridget felt the room begin to spin.

"A tent. Maybe two."

"I can cater!" Abby offered.

Margo seemed fine with this, and Bridget was too overwhelmed to reply. She tried to think of her upcoming reservation list, but she couldn't seem to think straight.

"We wouldn't need to stay at the inn. No out of town guests," Margo said. "So you wouldn't need to worry about a packed house. But I always wanted a backyard wedding."

They all did. It had been something they'd talked about since they were children, each putting their own spin on it. Instead, Bridget had eloped with Ryan, Margo had moved down south and had a big, church wedding of her mother in-law's dreams, and Abby...Well, Abby was happy keeping things casual.

"It will be gorgeous!" Abby was staring at Bridget now. "Won't it?"

Bridget forced herself out of her internal dialogue. "What? Yes. Yes, it will be beautiful."

"So it won't be a problem." Margo looked at her beseechingly, but Bridget couldn't speak.

A wedding here, in less than three weeks? How could that possibly be a problem?

But this was her sister. This was family.

And besides, if she was ever so lucky to be in Margo's position, she knew she'd want nothing but the same.

Not that she had time to think about dating or marriage. Life was complicated enough as it was, without having to worry about romance, too.

Chapter Seven

By the time Bridget picked Emma up from school and drove over to Serenity Hills, the worry must have been showing in her face. Emma had been quiet all during the car ride, but when they walked into the lobby of the nursing home, she took Bridget's hand and looked up, her eyes so earnest, it nearly broke Bridget's heart.

"Everything okay, Mommy?"

God bless her. Just hearing those words from that little face would make everything right every time, no matter what was troubling her.

"I'm just thinking," she said. That was an understatement. More like fretting. "Aunt Margo is going to meet us here, and she has some exciting news to share."

"Is she going to have a baby?" Emma asked, and Bridget laughed.

"No, honey." At least, she didn't think so… But no, Margo would have told her. They told each other everything, after all, and that was something to be grateful for. Not long ago, when Margo was living in South Carolina, they went for years without seeing each other and months without a phone call. Their lives had grown separate, and Bridget had gotten used to feeling alone, and having no one to lean on, especially when Mimi took a turn for the worse, but my, how quickly it became natural to turn to Margo now that she was back in town, and permanently, too.

Well, there was a perk to Margo getting married, she thought, brightening. With Margo marrying the newly appointed police chief, she surely wouldn't be leaving Oyster Bay again.

But she probably wouldn't be as available to Bridget as she had been recently, either. After all, Margo may not be having a baby now, but soon…

"You're frowning again, Mommy," Emma informed her.

"Am I?" Bridget forced a smile as she banished the long list of things she was telling herself she had to do. She'd checked in her newest guests, a young couple who were thrilled with Room One, a pretty room she'd done up in slate blue with white bedding, and Abby was insisting on handling breakfast tomorrow—Bridget was too distracted by Margo's announcement to argue with her. Still, just in case Abby was a no show or started an oven fire, she'd placed an order with Angie's for two boxes of pastries. Margo claimed that the wedding would all but plan itself, but Bridget knew otherwise. Margo would want the day to be special, and she deserved it to be, too. It was the first family wedding they'd ever had at the house, after all.

She looked down at Emma. And hopefully not the last, she thought.

She smiled again, more genuinely this time. "That better?"

"Much." Emma grinned.

After checking in at the front desk, they wandered down the hall to room 132, where Mimi had resided for just over a year now. In that time, Bridget and her sisters had done what they could to make it more comfortable for her, filling her room with all her favorite things from home, and inviting her out for dinner, or to the house for dinner, whenever she was up for it. But Mimi often declined these suggestions, given that the invitations didn't extend to Pudgie.

Bridget sighed. Why couldn't Mimi understand that it was bad for business when Pudgie marked the rugs and hissed at the guests? Honestly, she'd never seen anything like it. That cat was not an ordinary cat, that cat was—

"Lost!" Mimi's wail was audible through the partially closed door to her room.

Bridget looked down at Emma with wide eyes, then, tentatively, knocked twice on the door before pushing it open.

There, sitting in her wheelchair with her wedding quilt on her legs, was Mimi, looking more distraught than she had the time that the cafeteria ran out of her favorite dessert before she had a chance to grab a plate.

Beside her was Margo, who must have arrived earlier than planned, looking at Bridget in alarm.

"What's going on?" Bridget asked warily, suddenly wishing she could just turn around and go home. There was always something, it seemed, and oh, wouldn't it be nice to just take her latest J.R. Anderson novel down to the beach and escape for an hour or two?

"Pudgie's gone!" Mimi shrieked.

"Oh no!" Emma said, and immediately started to cry.

"Oh now." Bridget put an arm around her daughter. "He can't have gone far!" The building was large, but Pudgie rarely strayed far, usually just exploring the hallway before Mimi called for him to come back.

"He's only been gone for an hour," Margo added.

"See? He's probably exploring the building." Bridget gave Emma a little smile to show that everything would be all right.

"This room *is* awfully small," Emma said, after she'd thought about things for a moment.

"It's a jail cell!" Mimi declared, pinching her mouth. "No wonder my sweet boy wanted to escape! He should have brought me with him!"

And they were back to this. Whenever Mimi became agitated, Bridget and her sisters did what they could to change the subject.

"Why don't you go look for Pudgie, Emma?" Bridget suggested. "But stay in the building."

She chewed her lip as she watched Emma's blond ponytail swing behind her on her way down the hall. Was it possible that Pudgie had gotten outside? It seemed unlikely, and surely someone would have noticed?

"Have you asked around, Mimi?" Margo urged.

"We need the police," Mimi announced. "Someone call the police!"

Bridget and Margo exchanged a glance. "Why don't I call the front desk?" Bridget picked up the phone on Mimi's bedside table.

"Oh, I already did. They said he'll come back, but…" Mimi began to cry, and despite her personal feelings about Pudgie, Bridget felt her heart ache. She walked over and crouched down next to the wheelchair. "We'll find Pudgie, Mimi. He's here somewhere, and he can't have gone far. Let's go for a walk."

"No," Mimi said, sniffing hard. "I have to stay here in case he comes back."

"But don't you want to come to dinner? The dining room is serving your favorite tonight. Chicken pot pie."

"I can't think about food right now!" Mimi was shaking her head. "All I can think about is Pudgie."

Oh dear. No doubt Pudgie would be back at any moment. Still, Mimi had never reacted to Pudgie's wanderings. Bridget couldn't help but feel concerned.

"Do you want me to go look for him or stay here with

you?"

"No sense in us all sitting around," Mimi said. "You two go look. I'll wait."

"We'll bring you back some food," Bridget said sadly, hugging her grandmother good-bye. All the good offerings were gone by five, and the dining room opened at four thirty sharp.

She waited until they were in the hallway and out of earshot before turning to Margo. "What do you think?"

"Honestly? I'm worried. It isn't like that cat to be gone for more than a few minutes. If anything happens—"

Bridget held up a hand. She couldn't think about that now. Mimi had been through enough in the past year. "That cat means everything to Mimi right now. We will find it," she said firmly, even though she started to have a sinking feeling herself.

"Nothing can happen to that cat," she said firmly. It was one more worry she just couldn't take on right now. If Pudgie wanted to run away, he'd have to wait until the day after Margo's wedding, when Bridget would have time to find him.

*

Two hours later, and no sight of Pudgie, the girls decided to call it a night.

"I have to get Emma back to the house. She still has to do her homework."

"I'll go talk to Mimi," Margo said. "Hopefully he turns

up by morning."

They'd asked the front desk to review footage from the video cameras installed at the two exits of the building, but Bridget still hoped that the cat would soon grow hungry and come back. After all, Mimi was determined to spoil him with treats, even if it did make him tip the scales at twenty-eight pounds.

"Maybe they can give her something to help calm her down and let her sleep."

Margo nodded. "I guess I'll have to save my news for another day."

"What's the news?" Emma asked. "Are you going to have a baby?"

Margo laughed. "Not yet. But...someday." She grinned. "Actually, I will tell you, if you promise not to tell Mimi, so I can tell her myself."

Emma crossed her fingers and said solemnly, "I promise."

"Well, you know Eddie? My friend?" Emma adored Eddie. He was always telling her jokes and offering to play with her in the yard if Bridget and Margo were in the house. Once, she'd even roped him into a tea party. At the time, Bridget had laughed, but she also couldn't help but feel a little sad. There was no denying that Ryan was a part of Emma's life, and he was happy to take her on his appointed days, and he loved her, she knew he did, but Ryan had never been cut out to be a family man. And she had long since stopped trying to make him one.

There were some men who could commit, who

believed in things like family and love. And there were some men, who didn't.

Like Jack, she reminded herself. Another man devoted to his career.

When Emma nodded, Margo said, "He asked me to marry him and I said yes!"

Emma's eyes popped. "You get to be a bride?"

"I do," Margo said. "And I was hoping that you would be my flower girl."

Emma's smile was huge when she looked up at Bridget. "Can I, Mommy?"

"Of course!" Bridget said, thinking of how sweet Emma would look in a pretty white dress. Margo hadn't discussed colors yet, but a pale pink sash would look wonderful with the tulips that were still sprung around the porch. "And the wedding is going to be at the house."

"Wow." Emma soaked this in. "Two weddings at our house." She suddenly frowned. "But if it's our house, why aren't you the one getting married, Mommy?"

Margo glanced at Bridget and cocked an eyebrow. "Good question."

Bridget gave her sister a tiresome look that showed she wasn't up to this conversation again tonight. "As I said, we must go now."

"Tell Jack I said hello," Margo called after her, just before Bridget had safely escaped outside.

"Very funny," she said, but she couldn't help but perk up at the thought. Normally going home meant dealing with things like bath time and homework and packing lunch for the next day.

But tonight, it held a promise of something else. And despite all her reservations, her heart sped up at the thought of maybe seeing Jack again.

Chapter Eight

It was official: Pudgie was missing. Abby announced this with wide eyes and a slight tremor when she stopped by the inn the next afternoon with groceries for the week.

Bridget didn't know what dismayed her more: that her grandmother's beloved pet's whereabouts were currently unknown, or that she still hadn't had a heart-to-heart with Abby about the realities of this situation she'd never really agreed to.

"Why don't I pour us some coffee and we can talk about this..." Bridget hesitated. She couldn't call it an agreement, because it wasn't one. Struggling for the appropriate word choice, she settled on, "*Idea* of yours."

"Absolutely!" Abby nodded earnestly, and folded up the brown paper shopping bags.

Bridget inwardly groaned as she walked to the cabinets

and pulled two mugs from the shelf, which she slowly filled with coffee that had been warming on the burner since breakfast that morning. A breakfast that Abby had again prepared, but which, unfortunately, Jack had not attended.

When she turned to hand Abby her mug, she was surprised to see that Abby was already settled at a stool at the counter, a notepad in front of her, pen poised.

Oh brother.

Bridget willed herself to stay strong. Abby was known for fits of passion. She was a girl who followed her heart and always had, whether it came to men or jobs. But her heart was fickle, and she never stayed put for long. And that was one risk that Bridget just couldn't support, not when she'd taken on so much as it was by purchasing their childhood home from her grandmother and turning it into a business.

"Abby..." She swallowed hard, trying to summon the courage to tell her sister all the reasons this would not work, knowing that Abby would, as usual, be devastated for about five minutes and promptly move on. She'd seen it over and over: jobs that were her "dream job" that she quit three months later; men who were her "soul mate" whose names were forgotten within six weeks. Harper House Inn was no different. All it would take was one difficult guest, and Abby would be packing up her groceries, leaving Bridget in a lurch.

"As you know, I took on a lot of risk opening this place." She leveled her youngest sister with a look to drive home the gravity of the situation. "Every dime to my name went into this endeavor. I left my job as a real estate agent. My daughter's livelihood depends on me making this a success."

Abby nodded, but her eyes drifted slightly to her notepad and Bridget fought back a wave of frustration, wondering if Abby was even paying attention or just biding her time.

"When I promise my guests a service, I deliver. I have to deliver, because one or two bad reviews could have a big impact." Another reason to play it cool with Jack, she reminded herself. The man was her guest, and she didn't need any online accusations of coming across as needy or overbearing.

"So far, my guests have been perfectly happy with fresh pastries with yogurt and fruit. It's economical, and it's straightforward." And it never failed. Bridget hated to say it aloud, but she couldn't count on Abby. It wouldn't be long before one day, Abby just didn't show up, and then what? The bad reviews would pour in.

"Yes, but you could do better," Abby said. "I could do better." With that, she pulled a manila folder from under her notebook, and handed Bridget a typed sheet.

Bridget barely scanned the sheet. "What is this?"

"A menu!" Abby said excitedly, pointing to the first item on the list. "Of course, it's just my initial thoughts. If you have other suggestions, I'm all ears!"

Bridget fought back a sigh. This wasn't going to be as

easy as she'd hoped. Abby wasn't going to let it drop.

Until her passing whim had faded.

She skimmed the sheet, her eyes narrowing when she got to the last bullet point. "High tea?"

Abby's cheeks flushed. "It was just an idea. We can discuss it later, of course."

"Abby." Bridget set the sheet down and rubbed her forehead. It was time to level with her sister. "I'm afraid that I won't be able to offer you what you're looking for, financially. If you want a job in the kitchen, maybe you should talk to Uncle Chip—"

"I can't work at The Lantern!" Abby scoffed. "All that fish!"

Bridget tried not to laugh. When Abby's nose wrinkled like that, she looked exactly as she did when she was just five years old and expected to clean her room. Usually she whined and fussed until Bridget, the eldest and the most responsible, rolled up her sleeves and helped.

But this was one thing she just couldn't help Abby with.

"Abby, I really don't see how I can afford—"

"Oh, but I've figured it all out!" Abby pulled another sheet from the list. "These are your room rates. And here is what you could charge if you offered a sit-down meal, perhaps some light snacks throughout the day, maybe even a Sunday brunch or, uh, the high tea option."

Despite her reservations, Bridget humored her sister and looked at the figures. She expected to laugh out loud, or prove Abby wrong. After all, who was in the business?

She'd worked at the Oyster Bay Hotel as an assistant manager for years before becoming a real estate agent. She wanted to tell Abby that, believe it or not, she did know what she was doing.

Sort of. Some days, like the day the electricity went out with a big storm and she couldn't find any candles, she wondered if she had any business opening this inn at all.

"These are your rates and these are the rates at the Oyster Bay Hotel," Abby said.

Bridget had researched all this when she opened the inn, though truth be told, she had kept her rates a little low at first in order to garner business and a few good reviews. She'd hoped to eventually raise her rates when she'd gotten her footing. Now, looking at the figures, she wondered if the time had come.

"I suppose I could raise my rates a little," she said slowly.

"And things like high tea could be separate. There are all different ways to do it."

She wasn't going to let this go, Bridget realized. "Yes, Abby, but raising my rates and paying you are two mutually exclusive things. I have a mortgage, insurance, taxes, not to mention the upkeep of this place to think about."

"I don't need much! And I can always cater on the side for extra cash!"

"Cater on the side?" Bridget had only recently discovered that Abby liked to cook and bake at all, and now she was talking about catering.

Abby looked crestfallen. "But didn't you think I did a good job with the appetizers for the wedding?"

"Of course!" Bridget said honestly.

"And I'm going to handle Margo's wedding menu," Abby countered.

Ah, yes, that. Bridget hadn't had a chance to discuss this in private last night as she'd hoped; they'd been too distracted by Pudgie's latest stunt.

"An entire wedding menu is a lot for one person to take on," she pointed out, but Abby's mouth just firmed shut and her eyes took on an injured look.

"If you don't want me to help, just say so. I won't bother you again."

"Abby! That's not what I'm saying." But it sort of was, wasn't it?

Shame filled her when she thought of her childhood, spent here in this house, her mother in this very kitchen, packing up their lunches for school, her last words as they ran out the door were always, "Look out for each other!"

What would her mother think of her now? She was the oldest, and Mimi could no longer offer the advice and support she once had. Abby had lost her parents at a young age, when she was still in college. Bridget was all she had.

"I'll tell you what, why don't we do a trial run until Margo's wedding and see how the guests receive it. And as for Margo's wedding, we still need to go over more plans with her; at least I know I do." She frowned, wondering if a tent for the yard could even be ordered in such a short time frame.

Abby's face broke out into a huge smile as she flung her arms over her sister. "Oh thank you, Bridget, thank you! I promise, you won't regret this!"

Bridget's smile didn't match her sister's enthusiasm. She wasn't so sure about that.

*

With her afternoon chores wrapped up and an hour to spare before she had to pick up Emma, Bridget grabbed her sunglasses and novel and headed out the back door. The wind was chilly, but the sky was blue, and she watched the gulls swoop as she cut across the cool grass until she reached the beachfront, the best feature of the property.

She already anticipated the summer to be the busiest time at the inn, as tourists flocked to Oyster Bay for weekend getaways, and the private beach was a huge bonus, and a feature the Oyster Bay Hotel didn't have. Peak rates would apply, and maybe—she couldn't dare to stress that word enough—maybe having a warm breakfast and some other dining features would boost profits even more.

Still, with Abby's track record, she'd have to tread carefully.

Bridget pulled her cardigan tighter around her body as she reached the sand and bent to pick up the flip-flops she toed off. She straightened, about to head over to one of the Adirondack chairs for a few minutes of silence, when she saw him.

Jack.

He wasn't writing. Wasn't reading. Wasn't talking on the phone. He was just sitting there, staring out to the ocean.

She froze, not knowing what to do. A good innkeeper wouldn't intrude.

She was just about to back up when he suddenly turned and spotted her. Her heart flipped over when he held up a hand and smiled.

Oh, God. She had it bad. And that wasn't an option.

"Hello!" She smiled, having the distinct impression that it was one of those big, eager, toothy grins, not the more reserved ones she tended to offer to guests, and, following his lead, walked over to the row of chairs where he sat.

His shirtsleeves were rolled casually and his feet were bare under his faded jeans. A pair of shoes sat close by.

"Amazing view," he said, shaking his head.

"This is my favorite spot," she admitted, looking out on the crashing waves. "When I was a kid, my parents would have to pull us away, hose us down near the back porch before we were allowed entry."

No doubt she'd be doing the same this summer with Emma, she thought, grinning.

"How long has the house been in the family?" He looked at her with interest.

She eyed the chair beside him, and, after hesitation, sat down. Just for a minute. Oh, man. Up close she could see the flecks of gold around his pupils, the warmth in those otherwise impenetrably dark eyes.

She looked out to the horizon again. A safe choice.

"For generations," she explained. "It was my grandparents' house, and after my grandfather died, my parents moved in with my grandmother. My whole life was spent in this house, give or take a few years."

"And now you've opened it up to the public," he remarked.

She gave a small smile. "Yes. It's a business I enjoy."

"It can't always be easy, though. Not having any privacy."

"No." She had to agree. "But I find moments to steal away." She held up her book, then, remembering how he felt about romance in general, wished she hadn't.

Immediately, his eyes widened and something in his jaw shifted. Bridget felt her cheeks flush with heat.

"You like that author?" he finally asked, eyeing her sidelong.

Bridget frowned, wondering where he was going with this, if he was about to make fun of her, or launch into another argument about the realities of romance. "I do," she admitted. "She's my favorite author."

Something in Jack's face twitched, but he pulled in a breath and tented his fingers, looking out to the sea. Bridget used the opportunity to steal a glance at his profile. The strong jaw, straight nose, full mouth.

Her lids fluttered. *Look away, Bridget. Look far away…*

"How's your writing coming along?" she asked conversationally.

Jack raised his eyebrows and said, "Good. I've started to make progress." But instead of seeming relaxed, he seemed a bit agitated, at least if the pinch between his brow said anything.

"That's great!" She chewed her lip, wondering if she should ask more, but decided against it. Jack seemed extremely private about his work, and she didn't want to pry.

Instead Jack pointed to the book in her lap and said, "What is it that you like so much about that author?" After a pause he said, "Professional curiosity."

"Oh, I don't know." Bridget suddenly felt self-conscious. She was hardly in a position to critique a book to an actual professional, though she had plenty to say on the subject. "I suppose I like the fact that it lets me escape. Life can be rough, and these books give me a break from the everyday and allow me to imagine something just a little more…magical."

His eyes flickered and immediately she felt her cheeks flame. Magical! Why'd she have to go and use that word?

"Do you have a favorite book by this author?"

She narrowed her eyes at him, wondering if he was teasing her, but his face was expressionless and he stared at her, waiting.

"Oh, she's written over a dozen!" Bridget explained.

Jack's eyes briefly glimmered, but he didn't look surprised. She looked down at the sand, mentally skimming through all of those stories that had filled lonely nights and lonely days. The characters had felt like friends, family even, when she needed them the most. "I think my favorite was a book that came out about four years ago. It was about a man and woman who fell in love as pen pals." Now she was really embarrassing herself. After all, the man didn't believe in romance. He scoffed at weddings!

"You liked that the best of all this author's books?" Jack tented his fingers. "Interesting."

"Why is that interesting?" she asked.

"That this premise stood out," he said. "Two strangers, who sort of know each other, but...don't know each other's true identity?" He opened his palms, as if waiting for her to confirm.

"Exactly," she said, smiling. "I think that's what made it so exciting. The reader knew who they were, and the reader knew they were perfect for each other."

"But they didn't know it yet." He grinned, and oh, if her heart didn't start to race.

"Well." Bridget shoved the book to the side, deciding to forego her hour of reading. "I enjoy them."

"That's always nice to hear," Jack said, then, suddenly frowned. "I mean, as an author, it's always nice to hear when a reader enjoys an author's work. It's not always an easy job."

"I'd love to read one of your books sometime," she said.

"Maybe," he said, a little evasively. "But I am feeling a little inspired right now." With that, he pushed his hands down on the armrest and stood up, looming over her, his smile wan but lingering, and his eyes…unreadable. "Well, I suppose I should get back to it."

She swallowed, not wanting him to go but not knowing what else she could say about that, either. "I'll see you later," Bridget said, watching him walk back toward the dock that led up to the house, hating the tug of disappointment that lingered in her chest.

She pulled her book out and opened it to where her bookmark had last been placed, but she didn't read any of the words. Instead she looked out to the sea, at the very view Jack had just been staring at, and wondered if he might come down again around dinnertime…

Chapter Nine

Margo had asked for a meeting on Friday morning, and with only a bit of trepidation, Bridget agreed. The wedding was quickly approaching, and she felt lucky to have reserved one large tent and enough to house the fifty-guest figure Margo had mentioned on such short notice. Hopefully it would force Margo to stick to that number.

Abby was already sitting with Margo at their favorite corner table at Angie's Café, sipping coffee and pointing excitedly to something on her notepad. Margo looked up as Bridget approached with a look of amusement. "Abby's already planned the menu."

Bridget felt something in her stomach knot. She knew that Abby was excited about this. Now. But there was no predicting how she'd feel in a week or two. Bridget would feel a lot better about Margo's wedding if they were hiring outside caterers.

"Are you sure you want to take this on, Abby?" she said, as she sat down. "It's your sister's wedding. Don't you want to be a guest, not work the event?"

"You'll be working the event," Abby countered.

"Yes, but most of the work I'll be doing is in preparation for the wedding. By the time it starts, the job will really shift to the catering." And if Abby was handling that, no doubt, Bridget would have to pitch in, too.

"Not necessarily," Abby said. "I've come up with an idea for heavy hors d'oeuvres by station. Everything could be set up in advance, and since the weather is still mild, we won't have to worry about anything spoiling."

Bridget glanced at Margo, who seemed surprisingly on board with this suggestion, and looked at the notes Abby had on the table. She had to agree that this was a good idea—in theory.

She looked up at Margo. "It's your decision. Your big day."

"Abby did a great job with the Carrington wedding," Margo said. She grinned. "If you want to take this on, Abby, I won't stop you. God knows it will save a lot of money!"

True, all true. Still, Margo didn't see the sides of Abby that Bridget did. She had been living her own life in South Carolina, unaware of the endless stream of bad choices their youngest sister had made over the years, hopping from one job to the next, living day by day, without a plan.

Bridget literally tensed at the thought of it.

"Angie is going to make the cake," Margo announced, to Bridget's relief. "And for the dress…" Here she turned to them both, her eyes wide and a little hesitant. "I was wondering how you both felt about me maybe wearing Mom's dress."

Mom's dress. Bridget had almost forgotten it, and the endless afternoons that she and her sisters would spend in the attic as children, dressing up and standing before the full-length mirror, each taking a turn to play bride while the others were given roles like maid of honor or, often times for Abby, flower girl.

Their mother's dress was a classic. White satin with capped sleeves and a sweetheart neckline with a bodice that pinched at the waist and then flared out into a ball gown. A row of buttons down the back didn't disguise a zipper; no, those buttons were the real deal, and the girls would take hours pinching them through the holes, delighting in the finished product.

"I don't want to step on any toes," Margo continued. "We all loved that dress and we all have a right to it, and well, we're all single."

Gee, thanks, Bridget thought.

"And well, I didn't know if either of you had your heart set on it, for when you have your day."

Bridget pinched her lips, holding back the tug in her heart from registering on her face. She didn't dare think of another wedding day—or a real wedding, at that. She'd had her time. She'd had a family. She had a child. She was a mother now. That was her role. Not bride. Not even wife. It was just...reality.

"You should wear the dress," Bridget said firmly. "In fact, it's still in storage, and I even had it cleaned before we redid the attic."

Margo's face lit up. "Can I come by and try it on soon?"

"Of course," Bridget grinned. She swept her eyes over her sister's lean figure. "But it should fit. You're even the same height as Mom." Both were five foot five, whereas Bridget was an inch taller, and Abby was an inch shorter.

"The middle child in every way," Margo grinned.

"I wish Mom and Dad could be here for this," Bridget said, wishing when she saw the hurt in both of her sisters' eyes that she had kept that sentiment to herself.

"They're here in spirit," Margo said, blinking quickly. "It's our family home. And with how we're all pulling together, it's a family wedding."

Abby tapped her notepad triumphantly, and Bridget hid her concern the best she could. It was a family wedding. But as usual, it would be on Bridget to see to it that it was a success.

*

Jack didn't look up from his screen until close to dinnertime that night, alerted by the rumbling in his stomach and the sounds of other guests opening and closing their doors.

He looked at his word count. A lot to go but…not bad. If he kept up like this, he might just pull it off. *If* he kept it up…Familiar panic rolled through him, and he closed his laptop and stood, not wanting to think about it anymore.

He grabbed his room key and wallet and closed the door behind him. From the base of the stairs he could hear male and female voices, discussing dinner options, before closing the front door of the house behind them.

He went downstairs, knowing it would be too much to expect a second invitation to dinner, and wishing it wasn't. But instead of finding Bridget in the lobby or dining room, he saw her daughter instead, in the back conservatory, poised over a notebook, pencil in hand.

"You seem to be working hard," he observed, daring to steal a look at the notebook she had spread open before her.

"I have a homework assignment. On the weekend!" She said this as if it were the single most absurd thing she had ever heard in her life.

"Well, what's the assignment?" He tried not to smile at the stern look on her face.

"I have to write a story."

A story? He perked up at this. "Oh? What's yours about?"

"It's about my Mimi's cat. Mimi is my mommy's grandma," she explained. "And her cat got lost."

"Was lost? Or is lost?" God, listen to him. He sounded like such an adult. When did that happen? Last time he checked, adults didn't order takeout seven nights a week and frequently not bother to make their beds. Adults didn't stare at a blank computer screen instead of doing their job for months on end either. At least his own father hadn't. His father was an accountant. A numbers man. And Jack had been…a disappointment. Well, at least until he started earning real money for his work.

"He *is* lost!" Emma blinked rapidly and her chin began to wobble and something in Jack just turned to mush.

He dropped into a nearby chair. "Well. Let's take a look at this story. I happen to be very good at writing stories," he reassured her when she looked up at him skeptically.

"Really? Okay!"

He took the notebook she handed to him and began reading. "My Mimi's cat is very fat. And very spoiled too. This is probably why Mimi named him Pudgie."

Oh dear. He cleared his throat and turned his back slightly from the little girl, so she wouldn't see he was actually choking down laughter.

When he'd composed himself, he continued. "Pudgie likes to climb the drapes and wander the halls. Pudgie does not like my Aunt Margo. One time he scratched her and he hisses at her too."

He looked up and raised an eyebrow. "Is this true?"

Emma nodded solemnly. "Margo doesn't like that cat."

He turned the page. "Now Pudgie is gone and Mimi can't stop crying and everyone is sad. I am sad too."

Well, crap. Now Emma was crying.

Jack stood, bewildered, not sure what to do. He didn't grow up with his half-sister and he never spent time with younger children, especially as an adult. Did she need a hug? A pat on the head?

He looked around desperately for Bridget, not sure what she'd make of this. He'd made her child cry. Damn it.

"That's a great story!" he said. "But I bet we could make it even more exciting. You want to know how?"

Emma nodded, but continued crying into her hands.

Jack licked his lips. "Well, this is supposed to be a story, meaning you could make up parts. I think you could talk about Pudgie's adventure. I bet he's having one, after all."

Emma sniffed and looked up at him, her blue eyes watery and her cheeks pink. "Really?"

"Of course!" Jack said. "He's taking a big adventure right now. Exploring...maybe he chased a mouse!"

Emma giggled. "Maybe he climbed a tree!" She grabbed her notepad and turned to a fresh page, where she started scribbling something. "I'm going to call my story Pudgie's Big Adventure!" She held up the paper to show him, and Jack didn't know if he should point out that "adventure" was misspelled or leave it be. He decided to say nothing.

"I'm going to have him follow a mouse up a tree! Then, in the tree, he could meet another cat! And fall in love!"

Jack stifled a groan. Did it always come back to this? Boy meets girl?

He looked up at that moment to see Bridget standing in the doorway, her eyes soft with appreciation.

Yes, he thought to himself, he supposed it always did come back to this.

*

Bridget wasn't sure what she was more surprised by, that Jack seemed to be so engaged with her child, or just how much she had wished for a scene like this. A father figure for Emma, right here, in her home.

There was no denying the fact that Emma had a father. Ryan was usually good for his every other weekend visits, but more often than not, something came up for work and he had to cancel or reschedule. But it was the day to day moments, the routine of things as simple as bedtime stories and takeout meals that Ryan was missing.

"Emma was telling me that your grandmother's cat has gone missing."

Bridget blew out a breath, nodding. "Pudgie." That name was so ridiculous. "Yes, he is the apple of Mimi's eye. I'm afraid she's very upset."

"How long has he been gone?"

"Since Tuesday," Bridget said, thinking that this really wasn't looking so good anymore. "Everyone at Serenity Hills is looking for it."

"Serenity Hills?"

"Oh, the nursing home where she lives," Bridget explained. She shrugged. "All we can do is hope. I don't see how he could have gotten out. And he's so..."

"Spoiled!" Emma finished, laughing wildly.

Bridget couldn't help but laugh, too. "Mimi adores that cat and she'd given him a very good life. He has every motivation to come back to her." Which was what made it so strange that he was staying away for so long...

"I'm going to take her to The Lantern tonight to cheer her up," Bridget continued. "Speaking of that, Emma, you had better go change into your ballet outfit so we're not late for class. And bring a change of clothes. Daddy will be picking you up straight from the studio to take you to the movies." The plan had been in place all week, but Bridget couldn't help but hold her breath, waiting for a text or call to inform her that Ryan was busy at the restaurant and couldn't make it.

"The Lantern?" Jack asked, when Emma scampered out of the room.

"My Uncle Chip's restaurant. My sisters and I take our grandmother there once in a while. Chip was my mother's brother, but he's still like family to Mimi."

Jack's smile seemed sad. "Another family dinner, then."

Bridget wasn't sure if this was a hint at an invitation, but Jack didn't seem like the indirect sort. "We try. It's not always easy with our busy lives. If you like clam chowder, no one serves it better than Uncle Chip," she said, hating the edge of hope that lilted her voice.

"I might give it a try then," he said, backing out of the room as another guest emerged.

Bridget bit back a wave of impatience. Room Six was already becoming a bit high maintenance. Honestly, who ran through two bars of soap in one day?

"Well, I might see you later then," Jack said.

She nodded, and smiled long after he had gone, hoping that she would, until the stern gaze of the sixty-something Room Six guest forced her attention elsewhere, where she did her best to keep her smile polite and hospitable, even though her mind was racing with anything but professional thoughts.

Chapter Ten

Abby had spent the day experimenting with new recipes: the brioche French toast had been delicious, the vegetarian quiche not so much. Salt, she decided, as she sat down across from her grandmother and sisters at what had become their signature table at The Lantern, reserved just for them each time they came, which was about once a month, sometimes more. The quiche definitely needed more salt, but something else, too...

A good, sharp cheddar. Or feta. She'd try both, she decided. Still, given her budget and her current financial situation, she'd be living off the rather bland quiche for the next few days. Worse things had happened!

"Mimi, I have some good news," Margo said with a smile that almost seemed a little nervous. She held her hands together, her right hand covering the beautiful engagement ring that now resided on her left ring finger.

"You found Pudgie?" The joy in Mimi's face was heartbreaking, and the sisters exchanged worried glances.

"No..." Margo bit her lip, frowning. "I'm sorry, Mimi, not yet. But...I'm getting married."

Mimi frowned. "I thought you were married."

Oh dear. It was happening more and more, instances where Mimi was confused. She was always mixing Abby and Margo up, based solely on their similar hair color, and then there was the string of events that led to her having to move into Serenity Hills in the first place, the final straw being the time she left the stove burner on, which was discovered by Bridget when she stopped by to check in.

"I *was* married," Margo said slowly. She widened her eyes to Abby, then Bridget, for help, but what could they say? "But Ash and I...aren't married anymore."

Mimi folded her arms in her lap. "So two of my granddaughters are divorced then," she said loudly, causing the patrons of the nearby tables to turn to look at them.

Bridget fluttered her lashes and lifted her wine glass to take a long sip.

"Well, I'm getting remarried. To Eddie Boyd."

Surely Mimi knew Eddie. Not only was he the town sheriff, but he was also Margo's high school sweetheart.

"Well, it's about time! You two were so sweet together back in high school," Mimi explained, cracking her first real smile all week. "When is it?"

"Two weeks from tomorrow," Margo said.

"Two weeks!" Mimi shrieked, again drawing the attention of other customers.

"It's a small gathering. At home," Margo explained. Her smile looked a bit forced, as if she had somehow expected this all to go a little differently.

"At the inn," Bridget added, lest there be any confusion.

"And I get to cater the event!" Abby said, which seemed to make everyone's smile slip, just a bit. She shifted in her seat uncomfortably, all her old insecurities flooding back. With a shaking hand, she took a sip of wine, trying to restore her courage. She would show them. She thought she had once, but this time...she'd be sure.

"So it's a celebration of sorts," Bridget said, giving Margo a kind smile, and despite all the frustration Abby had built up for her sister, in moments like these, when Bridget stepped up and did whatever she could to please everyone else, she couldn't help but love her.

And maybe, miss her mother more than ever.

I'm going to make you proud, Mom, Abby silently pledged. This time she meant it, this time she would.

And it started with making Bridget proud. Because without her oldest sister's support, Abby couldn't help but feel like all her dreams were hopeless.

*

Jack pushed through the door of The Lantern, immediately taken in by the nautical theme and the cheerful din. The bar was to his right, and he walked over to it. In New York, he was used to eating alone, but here, in this small town, he felt out of place and conspicuous.

"What can I get you?" a guy behind the counter asked.

"I'll take whatever's on tap," Jack said, picking up a menu.

A moment later the man slid him a draft. "The name's Chip. Let me know what I can get you and I'll be sure you're taken care of."

"Chip. Bridget's uncle, right?"

Chip's grin showed that he was pleased by the connection. "That's right. You know my niece?"

"I'm staying at the inn," Jack said, but even as he said it, he knew that there was more to it, and he sensed that this Chip fellow did, too.

He did know Bridget. Or he was starting to. And it had been a long time since he'd gotten to know anyone. Or let anyone in.

And he wasn't so sure how to feel about that.

"Ah, well, if I know Bridget she's giving you the royal treatment then." Chip's eyes gleamed when he spoke of his niece, and Jack couldn't blame him. She was a nice woman. Smart. Pretty. Driven.

Right. He opened his menu and started scanning the appetizer list, but Chip wasn't done talking yet.

"In town for the Flower Fest?"

Ah, yes. The Flower Fest. It was all anyone could talk about, it seemed. Did people in small towns really like this sort of thing? He made a mental note to research this when he got back to the inn.

"No, just a change of scenery," he said.

"Bridget's probably booked full. I know the hotel is," Chip remarked as he refilled a water glass for the woman to Jack's left. "But then, I can't complain. She always refers her customers to me."

Jack scanned the menu, deciding on the chowder to start, and a burger for his main course. "I'll have to thank her then. It all looks delicious."

"Thank her in person, if you'd like. She's right over there." Chip jutted his chin and Jack turned to see Bridget sitting at a corner table with her two sisters and an elderly woman who must have been her grandmother.

Stiffening, he turned around. He'd taken her up on the suggestion, and maybe, maybe he had hoped to run into her. But he wasn't about to go over to her table. "I don't want to interrupt their family time."

"Nonsense! They'd be happy to see you. Besides, every day is family time around here," Chip pointed out with a grin.

Jack's own smile felt thin. He couldn't imagine that way of life, running into people he knew, stopping to chat at someone's table in a restaurant. In New York, he was free. Free to walk where he wanted and dine when wanted and go about his daily routine without risk of running into a single person he knew.

Sure, there were his neighbors. His walk-up was small, with six units in total. He recognized the lady across the hall. A woman in her sixties whom he knew liked to order Chinese takeout on Fridays and pizza on Sundays and who always left for work at eight and returned at seven. What she did for work, he didn't know. They exchanged pleasantries the few times they were stuck on the landing together, each eagerly fishing for their keys, but other than that, her world was her own and his was his own. He probably couldn't recognize the rest of the people in the building in a police lineup.

But here, in this small town, you couldn't go anywhere without knowing someone.

He wasn't so sure how he felt about that, either.

"Top you off?" Chip asked, eyeing Jack's half-finished beer.

Jack shrugged. He could say no, that he had to get back to the inn and work. And maybe that's what he should do. But tonight, he wasn't in a rush. Tonight he wanted to sit here, in this cozy pub with the ocean at his back, in a room where everyone knew everyone's name and probably their life story too.

Tonight, he wanted to lose himself in a fantasy, and not worry about reality or everything that had brought him to this point.

*

Bridget had barely started her main course when her

phone rang. She looked at the screen, knowing who it was without having to check, and not at all surprised to see that it was Ryan.

Margo caught her eye, looking displeased. "Do you have to go?"

Bridget felt her shoulders sink. The girls had finally lifted Mimi's spirits and she was having fun herself. Margo was making plans for the wedding, and this wasn't a conversation that Bridget wanted to prolong.

"I'll be right back," she said, pushing back her chair. She walked toward the front of the restaurant, waiting until she was away from the tables before connecting the call. "Ryan?"

"Hey, I hate to do this, but can you come get Emma a little early tonight?"

Bridget bit back a wave of impatience, and not because she didn't want to see her daughter. She had made plans, and now they would have to be altered, because, as usual, Ryan couldn't stick to his.

"I'm having dinner with my sisters and Mimi at The Lantern," she informed him. Dunley's was just down the street. From the noise in the background, this was where he currently was, even if he had promised to take Emma to see the new animated movie tonight. "If you can bring her by, I can place an order for her while I wait."

"Cool," Ryan said, and Bridget couldn't help but roll her eyes at the casual way he treated this situation. "I'll be there in ten minutes."

Ten minutes. Meaning more like five. She wondered what it was this time—bartender got sick and he had to stand in, or the cook's car broke down and Ryan had to roll up his sleeves. Or maybe Ryan just wanted to have fun. It wouldn't be the first time.

Bridget disconnected the call and shoved it into the back pocket of her jeans, her heart sinking when she thought of how disappointed Emma would be to miss the movie. She'd been chattering about it all afternoon, and now she'd have nothing to share with her friends at school on Monday.

She sighed and turned to the bar, hoping for a glance of Chip. He always cheered her up, sometimes just by listening, sometimes just by taking her mind off her troubles.

But tonight the person she saw wasn't Chip. It was Jack. He was wedged in the middle of the bar, a burger in front of him, and a half-finished beer in his hand. He was watching the TV screen. The Sox were up at bat. She idly wondered if he was Yankees fan, being from New York. If so, he'd be wise not to mention that to her uncle.

She glanced across the room, to where her sisters were eagerly talking, leaning across the table. No doubt Abby was menu planning.

She glanced at the door. No sign of Ryan yet.

She had a few minutes.

"So you decided to take me up on the recommendation after all," she said, coming up behind Jack.

Any worry she had that he might be annoyed at her interruption was put to rest when she saw the way his eyes shot up and his mouth curved into a big grin.

Her stomach flipped and fluttered all at once. Oh, Lordy. She had it bad.

"What can I say?" he grinned. "You convinced me."

"See, this town isn't so bad if you give it a chance."

"So I'm noticing," Jack replied, his gaze lingering just a touch longer than usual.

Bridget swallowed hard and licked her bottom lip, trying to think of something to say next and coming up completely blank.

"I'm waiting for Emma," she explained, realizing that she was hovering, and the man probably wanted to take another bite out of that burger in his hand before it went cold.

He gestured to his plate. "Fry while you wait?"

It was tempting. After all, Chip made the best steel-cut fries in town. She shook her head. "Our orders will probably be up by the time I'm back, but you just reminded me to place something for Emma." She craned her neck until she spotted Chip; he winked when he caught her eye. "Can I get Emma's usual?"

He nodded, without having to be told anything more. "I'll make sure it comes out with your order." Frowning, he said, "I thought Emma was with Ryan tonight."

Bridget's mouth thinned. "Something came up." Something always came up.

Chip gave her a knowing look. "I'll pass the word along to your waiter."

"Thanks, Chip. I can always count on you."

"Yes," he said. "You can."

Bridget felt instantly better, just as she always did when she was around Chip. Margo had that kind of effect on her too, and more than once a week she was thanking the heavens that her sister had returned to Oyster Bay, just when she needed her the most.

"And here's my favorite girl!" Chip announced as a breeze of salty air blew Bridget's back. She turned to see Emma and Ryan standing in the doorway. Emma looking tearful, Ryan looking sheepish.

She bit back a wave of exasperation. Once again, she would be left to clear up Ryan's mess.

"Hi, sweetie!" She beamed as she reached in to squeeze her daughter, even though she had only just seen her a couple hours ago. She couldn't help it; she missed Emma terribly on the nights Ryan had her. The hours dragged on and the house felt empty. It had always been this way, even before she opened the business and before she moved back into the big family home. Then she'd fill her nights visiting Trish and Jeffrey, admiring their cozy Colonial, wishing that life had taken a different path for her.

And now it had.

And it would all be okay. In a matter of minutes, Ryan would leave and Emma and she would rejoin her sisters and Mimi and soon all these lingering feelings that always came with seeing Ryan and splitting Emma would subside.

"Sorry about this," Ryan said, giving her a little smile.

Bridget maintained a stony expression. There were only so many apologies she could hear before she knew they didn't count. Still...Ryan wasn't all bad. There were times where he redeemed himself.

No, Ryan wasn't bad. But he wasn't an adult either. Ryan was like Abby. He lived by his dreams and changed plans on a whim. Maybe this was why she was so hard on her sister sometimes.

She softened a little, shrugging her shoulders. "Things come up. I understand." And she did, to a degree. After all, she had to miss Emma's first-grade class holiday party because she had a real estate closing that ran long. She'd never forgiven herself. Lay in bed that night heavy with guilt, and to this day felt on edge when any mention of a class party was released. Emma had forgotten about it. It was years ago! But not Bridget.

Something told her that Ryan wouldn't be losing any sleep tonight, though. That was the difference between them. And that, perhaps, was why it never could have worked out for them.

Ryan's shoulders seemed to relax at her change in demeanor and his grin broadened. Bridget looked away, focused on her daughter instead. It was still hard to look Ryan in the eye, even after all these years, and know that she'd tried, tried so hard, and that it hadn't been enough.

"I wanted to go to the movie!" Emma's lower lip began to quiver.

Now Bridget's smile had officially slipped. She gave Ryan a warning look. A look that said, "You had better make this up to her."

"I'll make it up to you tomorrow at the Flower Fest," Ryan told Emma, who looked only partially assuaged. "I'll get you an extra scoop of ice cream for dessert!"

Bridget rolled her eyes. If they weren't in a public place, specifically her uncle's restaurant, she'd have words with Ryan. This was his MO—he let Emma down and then tried to win her affection with sugar. Donuts, ice cream. Even candy.

"She doesn't need a stomach ache," she said with as much calm as she could muster.

Ryan's gaze was hard. "An extra scoop of ice cream never hurt anyone."

"Yes, but there's no need for—" She shook her head. She made a promise to herself a long time ago not to argue with Ryan in front of Emma, and she was breaking her own rule. "Forget it. We'll see you tomorrow at the Flower Fest. Eleven o'clock?"

Something in his eyes flitted. "Eleven. Sure."

Bridget felt a familiar twist of anxiety on behalf of her daughter. He couldn't let her down again. He wouldn't.

"Eleven," she said again, holding his gaze. "See you then."

She turned around to say good night to Jack before they headed back to their table, but the pleasant, easygoing expression on his face seemed to have been replaced with something a little more rigid.

If she didn't know better, she might just call it jealousy.

Chapter Eleven

The inn was full for the second weekend in a row, and Bridget had to admit, it was nice having Abby there to help out in the morning.

"How are we doing with coffee?" she asked, poking her head into the dining room to answer the question for herself. Every seat at the table was taken by a guest— mostly couples in town for a romantic getaway—but Jack had not yet come downstairs.

She contemplated bringing him up a tray as she lifted the empty carafe and carried it back into the kitchen, but then decided otherwise. The man was in town to work, and he knew what time breakfast was served. It wasn't her place to impose upon him.

It was her place, however, to make sure that another pot of coffee was brewed before guests got cranky.

Emma sat at the kitchen table, eating a blueberry muffin from Angie's, though Bridget noticed a croissant was on her plate, too. She smiled. The girl knew how to look out for herself, and heaven forbid the croissants all got eaten before she had a chance to snatch one.

Abby noticed her eyeing Emma's plate. "You know, you don't need to keep placing orders from Angie's," she said.

Bridget didn't want to point out that she hated to sever the relationship with the café lest Abby lose interest in this job one day soon. She had a good thing going with Angie's. They delivered right to the inn, and before seven thirty each morning, too.

"I don't think it hurts to have some pastries as an option," she said mildly.

"Why spend the money?" Abby pointed out. "Besides, I can make muffins, if that's what you want."

Oh, dear. Bridget started a new pot of coffee and gave her sister a sheepish smile. "I'm already committed to Angie's, so...I hate to take away the business."

"The business!" Abby scoffed as she began whisking eggs in a large bowl for another frittata. "Angie's is hardly struggling. It's always packed!" She muttered something about "despite their dry scones" under her breath.

"Well...I'll think about it," Bridget said, falling back on the excuse she always gave Emma when she was put on the spot and didn't want to make a decision one way or another, or really, didn't want to say "No" and have to deal with the fall out.

Abby just raised an eyebrow, looking unimpressed.

"What time is Daddy picking me up?" Emma asked, clutching her muffin with two hands.

Bridget looked at the clock. "In about two hours, honey," she said.

"Oh good! I'm going to wear my pretty flower dress," Emma announced, and pushed back her chair to scamper off before Bridget could call after to her to wash the blueberries from her fingers.

Bridget sighed and began clearing up Emma's plate. Feeling Abby's stare from across the room, she looked up to see her sister's cocked eyebrow.

"An entire muffin and scone gone to waste..." Abby clucked her tongue.

Bridget sighed. Honestly! "I'll save this for her for later."

The coffee had finished brewing, and Bridget was grateful for an excuse to leave the room. She poured the brew into the carafe and walked it back into the dining room, smoothing her shirt over her hips before she entered, just in case Jack had decided to surface.

But no. It was the same crowd. The two young couples, and the older couple, who held hands when they came down to breakfast that morning. Bridget couldn't help it; when she saw that, her heart felt almost heavier than it did the time her only guests were newlyweds.

"Ms. Harper," said the husband, as he stood to meet her at the buffet table. "May I have a word?"

Bridget felt her heart sink. It wasn't often that a guest complained, but when they did, it always felt like a personal attack. This inn was her home. The place where she'd grown up, the place she'd fought to keep when they all feared it may no longer stay in the family once it was confirmed that Mimi would remain in Serenity Hills. She'd sunk every dollar she'd ever earned into taking over the house and turning it into a business. It wasn't just a job. It was, well, a dream.

A dream come true, she thought with a smile.

"I'd like to talk about the breakfast."

And there went her smile.

Bridget felt her back teeth graze. She knew she should have listened to her gut. Abby wasn't a trained chef. She was a home cook. And all of this...it was another of her passing hobbies. So what, the eggs were raw? A shell had been found in the frittata? Heaven forbid a hair had turned up.

Bridget suddenly felt sick with dread.

"This breakfast is one of the finest meals I have had in quite some time," Mr. Lawry surprised her by saying.

Bridget's eyes shot open. "Oh. Well...thank you!"

"No, thank you!" Mr. Lawry said, grinning. "My wife and I travel quite a bit, and we always seek out country inns as opposed to stuffy hotels." He wrinkled his nose and peered at her over the rim of his wire-framed glasses. "I can tell you that your food is the best I've had in quite some time."

"My!" Bridget was momentarily speechless.

"Keep up the good service," he said, patting her arm, before he went back to the table.

Bridget's heart was racing as she walked back into the kitchen. It wasn't often she received a complaint from one of her guests, but in fairness, it wasn't often that one of them bothered to extend a compliment, either.

Abby caught her smile and looked at her suspiciously. "You're acting strange," she said, as she tossed some vegetables into the egg mixture.

"I just received one of the nicest compliments," Bridget said, walking over to the island. "And it was about your breakfast."

Abby's cheeks turned pink. "Really?"

Bridget felt a wave of shame, but only for a moment. Abby could cook, she was beginning to realize that. But could Abby commit?

"Keep up the good work," Bridget said with a grin, and went off to fold guest towels—a task she'd normally have to put off until after breakfast had finished, but not now that Abby was around.

She'd enjoy the perk while it lasted, she told herself.

*

There was rustling in the halls. Muffled conversations he could hear through the door, even though it was made of solid wood.

Jack pulled his hands from his keyboard and ran them through his hair. He was finally making progress, really getting somewhere, and he couldn't lose momentum now.

A door slammed in the distance. A woman laughed.

And Jack…lost his thought.

He sat back, cursing under his breath. It was fine, really. He'd been going at this for hours and a break was in order. A shower at the very least. And coffee. He checked his watch.

Of course. Everyone was at breakfast, starting their day. He half laughed when he thought of the way he'd look if he were to join them. Undershirt, jeans, a five o'clock shadow, and no doubt his hair was standing up in every direction. He couldn't go down like this. Not until he was presentable.

Right. He walked into the bathroom to start the water when he saw the towel at his feet, and another loosely draped over the shower curtain rod. The bathroom was in nearly worse shape than his perpetually unmade bed.

He should just take the DO NOT DISTURB sign off the door. Let the maid come in and straighten things up a bit. But he couldn't risk that happening when he was finally getting into the zone, tapping into that place that used to come so easily.

And so, it had come to this. He was out of towels. His room was in a worse state than his apartment. The surface of the desk was covered in papers and notes, and his suitcase was still open on the floor, his clothes spilling out. His bed showed signs of fitful sleep. And now he'd be forced to clean up before he even allowed anyone on staff here to change the sheets.

The noise in the hall had died down, and the few sounds he could make out told him that everyone was settled downstairs. Slowly, he opened the knob, keeping his body as a shield to any potential view of his room, hoping to make a quick dash to the linen cabinet at the end of the hall, when he saw her.

Bridget was standing all but two feet away, her smile guilty, if he didn't know better.

"Hello there," he said, wondering just how long she'd been standing there. And why. Weren't most of the guests downstairs, needing breakfast? Surely it was her busiest time of the day. And yet here she was. Standing in the hall. Looking so uncomfortable he could only assume there was a reason for her being here.

"Oh. Hello. I was just…" Bridget's eyes darted. "Do you need any soap?"

Jack studied her in amusement. "Soap?" So that was the excuse she was going with, huh? He'd had women invite him over for all sorts of reasons in his time: to kill a spider, to help assemble a piece of IKEA furniture. The intention was always the same.

His smile faded when he considered that Bridget's intention was far from offering him soap.

Bridget was sweet. And kind. And a single mother.

And he was…all wrong for her. All wrong for anyone.

"Or towels?" she tried. "Fresh towels. They're in the linen cabinet now. I was just restocking them…" Now her brow pinched as she seemed to catch sight of something over his shoulder.

Flinching, Jack shifted the weight on his feet until he could only hope that more of his torso was covering the view. He pulled the doorknob as close as he could without fully stepping out into the hall. Stepping out meant getting closer to her. And he couldn't do that. Shouldn't.

But strangely, it wasn't so much that he didn't want to.

"I'd love a set of fresh towels," he said, deciding to let her stop squirming and hoping that would send her off, away, where she couldn't see what a mess he'd made of her nice guest room or linger any longer, filling him with thoughts and urges he had no business to have.

She visibly exhaled as she smiled. "I'll bring those right over."

"No bother. I'll get them myself. Seems you have enough on your plate." He jutted his chin in the direction of the staircase, where from outside his room he could hear the clear buzz of the crowd in the dining room.

He already missed how quiet the inn was just a matter of twenty-four hours ago. And not only because it allowed him to think straight. Then it had just been him and Bridget. And Emma, of course. And now...he was one of the crowd.

"It's a full house, yes." Bridget blew a strand of hair from her forehead, but it remained firmly in place.

Without thinking, Jack reached out and brushed it away for her, his hand freezing when her eyes caught his.

His heart hammered in his chest when he realized how natural it had felt to do that, how familiar this house, and she, were becoming to him.

He dropped his arm quickly, then, just to be sure, shoved both of his hands firmly into his pockets.

"It smells delicious. Maybe once the crowd subsides I'll head down."

Bridget's gaze flickered. "Would you prefer me to bring you up a tray?"

He knew that room service—or family dinners, for that matter—were not part of the daily package he'd agreed to pay for. "I don't want to put you out."

"Nonsense," she said with a grin that was so friendly, he felt instantly at ease. "Abby's making frittata today. I'll get you a serving and a croissant for the side, if my daughter hasn't eaten the last of them."

He laughed. "She's welcome to it. She's a sweetheart."

"An excited sweetheart," Bridget said. "Flower Fest is today."

He rolled back on his heels. "Ah, yes. Of course. Seems that's all anyone can talk about."

"Why not come then? I don't know about you, but the fresh air always helps me to think."

"Maybe." He had to admit that the idea was becoming more attractive, and it would be interesting to see what the hype was all about. "First I'd like to try to get some work in."

"I'll leave you to it, then. Your tray will be outside your door in a few minutes."

"Thank you," he said, hoping she caught the sincerity in his voice, because he had a lot more to thank her for than just a meal or two.

*

Bridget had barely finished cleaning the kitchen—with Abby's help, which did make things run a little quicker—when Emma appeared in her favorite flower dress, pink sneakers, and a handbag whose strap she'd hooked crosswise over her body.

Her hair was brushed and her smile was nearly as bright as her eyes.

In moments like this, Bridget struggled to fight the heartache. Her little girl was eight years old. If she closed her eyes, she could still feel the weight of her in her arms as a baby, a toddler. She could still remember the way Emma wrapped her hand around Bridget's two fingers on her way into her first ballet class. And the way she giggled, straight from the belly, whenever Bridget read her favorite picture book aloud.

Now Emma read her own books. And she waved good-bye to Bridget on her way into school or dance class. How much time was left before that didn't even happen at all?

She walked over to her daughter, and without a word, gave her a long, hard hug.

"I'm going to miss you today," she admitted, even though she knew that Emma would be back by noon tomorrow, as designated by the courts.

"I'll get a flower wreath for you," Emma promised.

Bridget grinned, feeling better already. Emma may have grown, but she was still her sweet little girl. Bridget just hated to miss a moment.

"Did you pack your overnight bag for Daddy's?"

Emma nodded. "He's going to let me sleep in the tent."

"Inside the house, I hope!" Bridget hated this part of it. Not having any say in how Ryan chose to parent when she wasn't around.

"Of course, silly! There are bugs outside!" Emma wrinkled her nose, and Bridget laughed.

Really, she shouldn't worry so much. Ryan might be a bit casual when it came to his parenting standards, but Emma had a mind of her own, and one which Bridget happened to think was practically perfect.

"And what's in the bag?" She tapped the handbag that was stuffed so full, the purple zipper looked like it might pop.

"Oh, a coloring book. Some books. A few dollars from my piggy bank. An activity sheet..."

"Activity sheet?" Bridget didn't remember ever buying her one of those.

Emma was all too happy to retrieve it. "See?" She unfolded it, happy to present a used kids menu from Dagastino's Pizza Parlor on Main.

Bridget chuckled. "You're certainly resourceful." And, like herself, never one who stayed idle for long.

"Well, run and get your duffle bag and we'll head out soon," Bridget said, standing to grab her own bag. Her phone was wedged in the front pocket. A blue light was blinking in the corner.

Bridget felt her heart sink. She didn't need to look at the screen to know that Ryan had reached out to her. It was what she'd expected. What she'd known all along he would do.

What she hadn't wanted to believe. Just like she hadn't wanted to believe the dozens of other things that had led to them eventually splitting up—like the time he'd promised to take her out to dinner for their wedding anniversary, and hadn't even remembered to give her a card.

Her jaw tight, she pulled out the phone, tapped the screen, and stared at the message on the screen. "I can't believe this," Bridget muttered to herself.

"Everything okay?"

Bridget turned to see Jack frowning down at her, the warmth in his eyes almost undoing her. Bridget didn't do kindness. She hadn't been able to rely on it. She'd had to fight, every day, for the past eight years since her parents died and she left Ryan, to stay strong, to keep going, to not give in to the long days and setbacks and endless guilt and worry.

"Fine, fine." But she struggled to hold eye contact and her voice was thick.

"You don't sound fine," Jack observed as he set his

empty tray down on the counter.

No, she supposed she didn't. For the second time in two days, her little girl would be let down, and there was nothing she could do to change that.

"It's nothing," she said, only then realizing that she was fighting back tears that burned warm. She hated herself for giving in. For letting Ryan hurt her. For crying over something that she had no power to stop. For wanting something that could never happen. That hadn't been for her.

A traditional family. A childhood for Emma much like the one she'd had. She was halfway there, bringing Emma home to this house, but the rest of it...It wasn't what she'd planned. It wasn't what she'd wanted.

"Hey." Jack's hand was warm and steady on her shoulder, his grip reassuring and showing no sign of moving.

Bridget wiped her eyes, but the tears fell faster than she could stop them. "It's...it's Emma's father. He was supposed to take her to a movie last night and instead, he dropped her off early. She was so disappointed." She sniffled hard, her eyes darting to the hallway that led to her living quarters. She couldn't let Emma see her like this. "He promised to make it up to her today. At the Festival. But he just texted he's going to be late, and...I won't be surprised if he cancels altogether."

Jack swore under his breath. "I'm sorry, Bridget. I wish there was something I could do."

Bridget shook her head. "There's nothing anyone can

do. Not even me. I try so hard to give her the life I always dreamed for her, and..."

"I'm ready!"

Bridget turned to see Emma standing in the kitchen entry, her duffle bag at her feet, her stuffed unicorn (a gift from Ryan for her eighth birthday) in her arms.

Oh, God. As usual, it would be Bridget left to deliver the bad news. Bridget left to deal with the heartbroken confusion that always filled Emma's eyes, and the tears that inevitably followed.

"Honey, there's been a change of plans—"

"There has," Jack said, his voice loud and firm. Startled, Bridget looked up at him. "Your mother here has been talking about this Flower Festival all week. I didn't think it was possible, but I'm almost thinking it might be fun. That is, if you wouldn't mind showing me around a bit. Maybe be my tour guide?"

Emma's eyes widened in delight. "I can do that! But..." She looked at Bridget for approval. "Will Daddy be waiting?"

Bridget waved a hand through the air. "Oh, I'm sure he'll understand this once. Maybe we can meet up with him later." *If he keeps to his latest promise.*

"Then it's a plan?" Jack asked, glancing at her sideways.

Bridget had to swallow the lump in her throat before she spoke. "Yes," she said, sighing gratefully. "It's a plan."

The best plan she'd had in a long, long time.

Chapter Twelve

Margo and Eddie had already found Abby and Mimi when Bridget spotted them near the May Pole at their designated meeting time. Bridget wasn't sure who her sisters looked more surprised to see: Emma or Jack.

Jack, she decided, noticing the way Abby had to bite her lip as she stared at him and then back at Bridget.

Before either of them could comment, she said, "Emma isn't meeting up with Ryan until later, after all, so she decided to show our guest what all the fuss is about."

Abby looked about as unconvinced as Margo did pleased. "Nice to see you again, Room Four," Margo joked. She linked her arm through Eddie's. "This is my fiancé, Eddie Boyd."

"They just got engaged this week, and I get to be their flower girl!" Emma said excitedly.

To his credit, Jack gave a thin smile. "Congratulations. When's the big day?"

"Two weeks from today," Margo laughed, and Bridget felt that familiar flutter return. Two weeks and so much to think about! They had to discuss linens...of course...and tables! She still had to rent tables and chairs! "We're having it at the inn."

Jack raised an eyebrow in her direction. "Another wedding at the inn?"

She felt her face heat at the mere mention of that night they'd...Well, no use thinking about that. Much as she wanted to.

"Have you seen much of the town?" Margo asked Jack.

He shrugged in return. "Not enough of it, probably."

"Maybe Bridget can show you around!" Abby volunteered with a toothy smile, and Bridget had to shoot her a warning look. She glanced at Jack, to see if he was as horrified as she was, but he seemed to be fighting back a smile, and determined not to look her in the eye.

Sensing her embarrassment, and ever the peacemaker, Margo kept the conversation going as if Abby had never interrupted.

"Well, be sure to stop by the Clam Shack before you head out of town. It's down at North Beach, and don't let its appearance turn you off." She laughed.

"I'll make a point of it," Jack said, and something in the way he grinned made Bridget think he would follow through.

This town was growing on him, she thought. Or maybe…the people in it?

Nonsense. She was the innkeeper. And…the woman he had kissed.

They did a lap of the festival, letting Emma run ahead at times and stop to play a carnival game at other times. At Emma's insistence, they dropped off her hat, which would be used in the hat decorating contest Emma would enter later in the day. Eventually they circled back, in search of shade and a cool drink, but not before bumping in to Trish and Jeffrey.

"My old work wife," Jeffrey joked, when Bridget hugged both her friends.

"Jeffrey and I used to work together before I opened the inn," she explained to Jack. She glanced at Trish, whose eyes were dancing.

"I remember you from the bookstore," she said.

"That's right," he said. "Nice little shop you have."

"Thank you! And how long are you in town for?" Trish was clearly eager for information that Bridget had purposefully not shared, but Bridget couldn't help but love her for it. This was her oldest friend, and she just wanted what was best for her. Even if Trish did think that was finding Bridget a man.

The right man…that wouldn't be so bad.

"Another week," Jack replied, looking down at Bridget briefly.

One more week, she thought. Then…

"In town for vacation?" Trish pressed.

"A change of scenery," Jack replied. Bridget waited to see if he would elaborate, but he seemed to have nothing more to say about his reasons for being in Oyster Bay.

"Well, you're staying at the best inn, with the best innkeeper," Trish said, and this time, Bridget did have to roll her eyes at her friend's obvious tactic.

But to her pleasant surprise, Jack just said, "I've come to realize that."

Well, now Trish was simply beaming. Noticing that Bridget had had just about enough of this, Jeffrey decided to spare her, and, giving her a little wink, he took his wife by the elbow and led her toward the food trucks.

"I wonder if Trish carries any of your books in her store," Bridget wondered aloud.

Jack's jaw seemed to tighten. "Maybe."

"I think that man is winking at you, Mimi," Abby said, interrupting Bridget's thought process and causing Margo's eyebrows to shoot up.

Mimi frowned. "What man?"

Margo exchanged a glance with Bridget, her eyes sparkling. "Yes, which man, Abby?"

Abby rolled her eyes. "Well, you don't need to all be so obvious about it." She swiveled Mimi's wheelchair around and darted her gaze to the left. "Blue shirt, khaki pants. Bow tie."

"Wouldn't a bow tie have been enough?" Margo pointed out, as the entire group less than subtly turned to stare.

"Oh, he's cute!" Bridget exclaimed, when she saw the elderly man sitting on the bench, wiggling his eyebrows in Mimi's direction.

"Pfft!" Mimi exclaimed, but she looked secretly pleased if the pinched smile she was doing a poor job of fighting said anything.

"Do you know who he is, Mimi?" Oh, dear, Bridget thought. Now he was really grinning. And yep, there was a wink.

"No!" Mimi looked away, but after a moment, glanced back in the man's direction. "Well, maybe he's new. His relatives probably dumped him the way you dumped me!"

And here it came. Bridget felt the familiar tug of guilt, but Margo was there to step in, thankfully.

"Now, Mimi, if I didn't know better, I might say you had an admirer."

Mimi's eyes seemed to widen on that thought.

"We can go over to him if you'd like," Abby added, already pushing the chair across the grass.

Mimi slapped at the armrest, forcing Abby to stop walking. "No, no. I'm here with my family. Free from that jail for a day. I'll see him later. Back at home."

Home? All three sisters' eyes burst open on that word. Mimi had never called Serenity Hills home before, and they quickly recovered, desperate to act natural and downplay the wording lest she correct herself.

"Well, it's fun just the same. Maybe if you'd like, I can paint your nails tonight," Abby suggested.

"Maybe," Mimi said, looking down at her hands as she fought off a smile.

"I should go find Ryan," Bridget sighed, looking down at Emma. She said a silent prayer, hoping that Ryan was where he'd said he would be at this time.

"Want some company?" Jack asked, and Bridget felt momentarily conflicted. These interactions with Ryan were always tense, even if they were both trying to work on getting along for Emma's sake.

"It's probably easier if I go alone." She tipped her head, deciding to go for it. "But I wouldn't mind some company after."

There was one, heart-stopping moment before Jack grinned. "I'll be right here."

*

Jack was sitting on a bench under a maple tree when Bridget returned a few minutes later, relieved that Ryan had shown up this time, and that the plan for Emma to spend the day at the festival and then spend the night in the tent he'd set up in his living room was still in place.

For now.

But for now, she thought, as a flutter of nerves took over, she would enjoy the day. And that seemed to include plans with Jack. She'd idly wondered if he'd head back to the inn now that his kind gesture to ease Emma's disappointment was fulfilled.

"I'm supposed to tell you that Margo and Eddie went to check out the flower arrangement contest, and Abby went home to...experiment with recipes?"

Bridget blushed, realizing she had been so happy to see Jack she had barely given the rest of their group a thought. "Right. Good. And my grandmother?"

Mimi might still have most of her wits, but she was in a wheelchair, and in no position to be moving around the festival on her own.

"One of the workers from Serenity Hills brought her and that man in the bowtie over to the gazebo to see the folk concert. Margo said a bus would take them all back in time for dinner."

That meant that everyone was accounted for. And busy. And that she and Jack were on their own.

"Do you have to get back to write soon?" She held her breath, unsure of what he might say, and tried to think of an excuse for how she would keep busy, especially now that Emma was gone.

She did have laundry to do. And a house full of guests that she couldn't ignore. And she did want to spend a bit more time with Trish and Jeffrey before heading back...

But she also wouldn't mind extending her conversation with Jack a little longer.

"The writing can wait." He stood, grinned, and said, "Hungry?"

"Famished," she admitted. She hadn't had anything to eat all day but half a croissant, and that had been hours ago. Not sure what he had in mind, she tilted her head toward the food stands. "We could see what they have?"

They joined the crowds and perused their options, settling on lobster rolls and iced teas, and found a shady spot under a tree.

"So what do you think of the Flower Fest?" she asked.

Jack took his time before answering, savoring a bite of the lobster roll. "They make a mean lobster," he said, and she laughed.

"Hey, we are in Maine," she pointed out.

"Everything better with you and Emma's father?" he asked, looking her in the eye, his expression sobered, maybe a little concerned.

She pulled in a breath. "Yes. Well, as good as it can be. I was young when I married him, and…well, blind, I suppose. We didn't want the same things, and I refused to see that." She didn't want to bore him with all the details, and she didn't want to spend her day thinking about them either. "He cared more about his work than me," she said, summarizing it.

A shadow seemed to fall over Jack's face. There was a moment of silence before he said, "That couldn't have been easy."

She shook her head, her heart heavy when she thought of that time in her life. She never wanted to go back to it again, a feeling of loss and hopelessness and struggle. "It wasn't. And I waited it out, thinking he would change, but…people don't really change, do they?"

Jack looked down, pondering this. "Once I might have said no. But, maybe?"

Bridget felt her jaw slack. "That's so optimistic of

you!" she said, laughing.

He laughed too. "What can I say? You're turning me into one." He grinned, and she felt her stomach flip over. "So tell me, how is it that you still believe in love and romance and all this stuff after that?"

"I didn't, at first," she admitted. "But then, well, I dared to think that there was a chance that someday things might still work out the way I had hoped."

"Why the change?" he asked, his alert eyes genuinely interested.

She felt her shoulders deflate, wondering how he would react to her response. "Honestly? There's this author I like. The book I had on the beach."

He didn't say anything, just stared at her. "Really." It was a statement, not a question, but he wasn't laughing, and that was something.

"I know it's just fiction, but those books made me feel like good things can happen. That people can connect. That they can even fall in love. And that, well, they can live together, happily. Forever."

Now Jack's face was all ruddy, but she couldn't make out his expression—a strange cross between horror and disappointment.

"Anyway, it probably sounds silly," she said.

"It doesn't sound silly," he said softly. "It sounds...nice."

"Maybe you'll find the same sense of hope one day," she said. She hesitated, then decided to continue the conversation, since he was the one who had turned it personal. "How long were you married?"

"Ten years," he replied matter of factly. "Divorced for three. She...she remarried. About a year after we split."

Ah. "That couldn't have been easy." She had secretly worried about Ryan remarrying, at first, when they'd split. Then she realized that Ryan wasn't the marrying kind— then or now. There would be women in his life, but they wouldn't mean much. Just like she probably hadn't meant much, either. At least, not enough...

"Yeah, that was hard, I won't lie. Almost worse than the divorce," he said, giving her a secret smile.

"You loved her," she observed, not finding any jealousy in this statement, but rather, again, hope. It was in there, somewhere. A soft spot. A romantic. A believer.

"I did," he said. He blew out a breath and crushed his paper bowl into a ball. "But, it's over now. And now I know."

"What do you know?" she asked, standing to help him clear their things. She waited for him to say something cynical and biting.

Instead, he said, "Now I know that's over. And once, not too long ago, I might have left it at that."

"And now?" She stared at him, wondering what he would say.

"Now, I see that you can't plan for everything. You have to take the good surprises with the bad."

"I should take that advice, too," she admitted. "I guess I take myself a little too seriously at times."

He was staring at her, so intensely that she had no choice but to look up. His eyes were blue as the sea in the afternoon sun, and she tried to look away but found that no matter how much she wanted to, and how much she probably should, she couldn't.

"I had a really nice time today," Jack said.

Her pulse skipped. "I did too."

"I've had a really nice stay in general." He gave a boyish grin, just like he had that first morning when he appeared in her dining room. "I didn't plan on that."

The old Bridget would have felt nervous and stiff and gotten all red in the face and flustered, but Jack was right: today had been nice. And so had this week. And just for the moment, this was all she was going to focus on. "Well, as you said, sometimes life throws us a nice surprise."

And it had, she thought, smiling to herself.

*

Jack could have spent the entire day with Bridget, walking around the festival, talking, just enjoying her companionship. But they both had work to do, and it couldn't be put off all day.

"Well," Bridget sighed, as they pulled to a stop on the gravel driveway that led right up to the big old Victorian house, "I hope you found some inspiration for your work today."

"I'm sure I did," Jack said, as he reached for the door

handle.

"What's the name of the book you're working on?" she asked, as she fell into stride beside him.

"No title yet," he said. Really, it was the least of his worries. His editor could turn to the marketing team for a title. But it was Jack who had to come up with the words, the story. No one else could do that job for him, much as he wished he could pull in some help. "I'm still working out the plot for now."

"Stuck?" Bridget asked.

He was about to say yes, that he hadn't written in months, that he spent his days either staring at a blank screen or dodging the task altogether by roaming the city and avoiding his apartment, until he realized that this wasn't completely true anymore. Lately, since coming to Oyster Bay, the words had been flowing from him, and the ideas were popping so quickly, the first page of the notebook he kept by his side was filled with scribbles and lines and thoughts he didn't want to lose. It wasn't a chore to sit in front of his computer. The hours ticked away, his mind faraway; deep in fiction, his mind was alive.

How long had it been since he could say that?

Too long. Way, way too long.

"After my divorce, it was hard for me to write," he admitted. "I got a little lost, I guess you could say."

"I can understand that," she said, giving him a faint smile. "It shakes up your entire world. It's like moving backward at the same time you have no choice but to move forward."

"Exactly," he said, blinking. He'd never thought of it that way, but yes. It was a lot of pressure. "I tried to sit and work, but...nothing." Blank. His mind had been blank, where once it had been filled.

Bridget nodded. "When Ryan and I split up, I kept misplacing things. My car keys, my hairbrush...I would go to the grocery store and come home without the one item I went there to buy."

He couldn't help but laugh. She understood. She genuinely understood.

"How'd you get over it?" he asked, curious to know. Was there a magic cure? If so, why hadn't he found it?

"I had Emma. I have no choice," she said, looking up at him.

He felt a bit of shame. Here was a woman who had no choice but to push through and keep going, where as he...he hadn't moved forward at all, had he?

Until now.

"But I guess I was lucky, right?" Bridget said. "I had Emma, and it forced me to have to think of someone else, other than myself, which was hard...really, really hard...but...I also had someone to love. And someone who loved me. I wasn't alone, not really. So really, I was lucky. *Am* lucky," she stressed, with a grin.

In the late afternoon light, her blue eyes were as bright as the sea, and her smile was radiant, broad and heartfelt, causing her eyes to crinkle at the corners. Jack felt something in him pull. A need. A desire.

He looked away.

They were at the steps now, and soon they would be inside, and he would have to go back to his room and open his computer and immerse himself in a fictional world. Once, he liked nothing better than that. But lately, since coming here, he preferred real life for a change.

"The stories didn't help you escape from your troubles?" Bridget looked hesitant. "But then, I suppose writing a story is much different than reading it."

"Much," Jack attested. He shook his head as he took the porch steps, slowly. "I blamed my work for my divorce. At least...that's what Erin had done. And maybe she was right. I was so caught up in the stories that I was creating that I'd lost my own along the way."

He hadn't paid her enough attention. Hadn't put her first. That's what she'd said, at least. And maybe it was true. He wasn't living in the present. He was living in his fiction, his own, internal world that she hadn't been a part of, even if she was. She'd been a part of him. But he hadn't been able to show her that. He'd failed her. Failed them both.

Bridget was frowning, and for a moment, he couldn't help but feel like he'd somehow let her down, just as he had Erin. He'd put work ahead of his wife. And he hadn't even realized it.

"At least you recognized that," Bridget said, giving him a small smile. "Some people never do."

"I only realized once it was too late." He shook his

head. "Then...I guess I came to resent writing. I fell out of love with it, you might say. Nothing about it mattered, and the stories I was supposed to be telling didn't seem real, or from the heart. I would sit at the table with every intention of working, and just nothing would come out."

"What did you do?" she asked.

What he had to do, in the end. He was under contract, not delivering the manuscript wasn't an option, not when he'd already been given an advance he couldn't afford to pay back. "The last book I published was an old manuscript. One I dusted off and polished. But now...now I have no choice but to produce something." And soon, he thought, feeling that familiar knot resurface. He was on his way, but he still had a long way to go. And he didn't fully trust himself, not yet. He was shaky, out of sorts, and treading slowly. He needed to stay sharp, not let himself slide back into that dark place.

"I'd still love to read your work," Bridget said with a grin, and Jack felt immediately uneasy. He'd said too much, piqued her curiosity, and he didn't want that.

What he wanted, he realized, was this...This casual way of chatting they'd developed. This easy banter. He wanted her to know him. Not his words. Not his work.

Not the man he used to be.

"Well, here we are," she said as they walked into the front hall. No guests were in the lobby, and Jack assumed that everyone was still at the festival, and might stay in town through dinner. The house would be quiet, giving him a chance to sit and concentrate.

"Thank you," he said, stopping at the base of the stairs.

"For what?" she said, looking up at him with interest, her blue eyes twinkling.

For everything, he wanted to say. But his mouth felt dry. The house was too quiet. Especially for an inn. And he was overly aware that they were alone, and that all he wanted to do in this moment was the very thing he'd done the first night he'd met her, and that was to kiss her.

His gaze lingered on her mouth, on the full lips that were slightly parted, and he leaned in, slowly, his eyes starting to droop as he neared her. She didn't back away, didn't move, and his pulse was drumming fast, making him feel more alive than he had felt in years.

And then...sunlight. Pouring in. And voices. The front door was open, an elderly couple was shuffling inside, and with a secret smile in his direction, Bridget backed away to greet them.

Jack retreated to his room, telling himself that maybe it had been for the best.

Only he wasn't so sure about that anymore.

Chapter Thirteen

Abby arrived at the inn at seven sharp and gently set the brown paper bags of ingredients on the floor of the back porch as she let herself directly into the kitchen. She'd hoped to have a few minutes by herself to get started on prepping this morning's recipe—blueberry shortcake with fresh cream and a potato quiche for those looking for a savory option—but Bridget was already dressed and sitting at the kitchen island, sipping a mug of coffee.

Several white bakery boxes from Angie's were stacked beside her. Abby pinched her mouth and moved the boxes to the side as she set her bags down.

"Good morning!" Abby said cheerfully as she began unloading her ingredients. She kept glancing at the bakery boxes, half-wanting to say something again, half-angry that Bridget still insisted on a fall back, but managed to refrain, even if it did take every ounce of patience out of her.

She glanced at her sister, who still hadn't returned her greeting. Bridget seemed suspiciously far away, and it wasn't until Bridget followed her gaze that she noticed the beautiful lace wedding gown hanging by the back of the door that led to Bridget's personal quarters. "Oh," she breathed, taking it in. "Mom's dress."

She had to admit that it was even more beautiful than she'd remembered it. When they were kids, they'd admired it, even begged to try it on, but back then all wedding dresses had seemed beautiful, and all had pretty much looked the same. Now on closer inspection, she saw the quality of the cut, the richness of the material.

"It's stunning."

"It really is," Bridget agreed. "I told Margo I'd bring it over after I pick Emma up from Ryan's."

"I hope it fits her," Abby said, turning to reluctantly pull her items from the bag. It was such a pretty dress, she could have admired it a little longer. But…duty called.

"Oh, it will." Bridget smiled, but she seemed distant and not quite herself.

Stress, Abby decided. Bridget was always sweating the small stuff, like what time Emma went to bed, or doing laundry, or making sure that Mimi took her blood pressure medicine. And who could forget her anxiety over the matching socks! Honestly. If anyone asked her, which no one ever did, she'd say that what Bridget needed was to take a step back and stop trying to control everything.

"The wedding is in less than two weeks now," Abby said, wondering if this might prompt Bridget to express her feelings. She almost laughed as she pulled a whisk from the drawer. As if that would happen. Bridget was tight lipped. Always had been. Admitting she had concerns would be admitting she wasn't in control.

Oh, she'd express her stress, of course. Time! Time was always an issue to Bridget. But her real, inner feelings?

They were a mystery.

"Is it?" Bridget looked momentarily confused and Abby set down the whisk. Okay, something was definitely wrong. The sister she knew would have known not just how many weeks, but how many minutes until the wedding. Especially since she seemed to think she was responsible for it, even though this was still all their home; at least, Abby thought of it that way.

Since Bridget had bought it from Mimi and turned it into an inn, more had changed than just Abby's childhood bedroom.

"Thirteen days, actually," Abby said. She eyed her sister carefully. Bridget didn't even flinch. "I was thinking of wearing my chartreuse halter dress."

"Hmm." Bridget sipped her coffee, staring randomly at the stainless-steel fridge behind Abby.

"Maybe I'll get a tattoo, too. And bleach my hair."

Still nothing.

Exasperated, Abby set down her whisk, loudly. "Okay,

what's up?"

Bridget blinked and had the nerve to play dumb. "What do you mean?"

"I mean, that I just said I planned to bleach my hair and wear chartreuse to our sister's wedding and you didn't even notice."

Bridget blanched. "You're not serious, are you?"

Abby's lips thinned. Yep, good ol' uptight Bridge was back. "Obviously not. But it's nice to know I don't have your approval if I was serious." *Not that I need it*, she said to herself. She was nearly thirty, after all. When was Bridget going to open her eyes and notice that?

Bridget shook her head. "I'm sorry, Abby. I didn't get much sleep last night."

Well, that was interesting! "A long night with…Room Four?"

Bridget laughed, but the blush in her cheeks gave her away. Abby felt her heart soar and sink all at once. She'd hoped for years that Bridget would move on, find a good guy, someone who would treat her a lot better than that jerk Ryan Dunley ever had. But even if something was happening, even if Bridget had feelings, they weren't to be shared.

Abby wasn't in the sharing circle. She wasn't a confidante. Nope. Bridget had Margo for that.

"I suppose I should start some coffee in case any guests rise early," Bridget sighed, dragging herself from the bar stool. She was wearing a lower cut sweater than usual, in a shade of blue that Abby had always told her brought out the color of her eyes, and her best jeans.

Yes, interesting. Quite interesting indeed.

"What?" Bridget asked, turning to look at Abby with narrowed eyes.

Abby blinked innocently, and began whisking the cream faster than needed. She stopped, before she curdled it. "Nothing. Just...making my dish. Don't you have some coffee to make? For the guests?"

Bridget hesitated, but said nothing more as she went about making the coffee.

"I was thinking I might visit Mimi later on," Abby said. "You can join me if you'd like."

She half hoped that Bridget would say no, that this would force her hand, prompt her to reveal other plans she might have for the day...and why she was dressed nicer than usual.

Instead Bridget pressed a few buttons on the coffee machine and said, "Sure. I'll bring Emma. She'd like that."

Abby sighed. So much for getting any information out of her sister.

Maybe she'd try the other one...

*

Thirteen days until Margo's wedding. Thirteen days until all their friends and family in Oyster Bay gathered in the house, where, no matter what Margo insisted, Bridget would be hostess on duty.

She should be making lists, scratching things off, collaborating a bit more with Margo, nailing down a hard schedule from Abby. Thirteen days! What was she thinking?

But she wasn't thinking. Not about the wedding, at least. She was thinking about Jack. And how he'd almost kissed her. Again.

She closed her eyes after she turned the ignition off in front of Margo's cottage. When Margo had moved back to Oyster Bay, she'd rented this small, seaside cottage by the week, but once she decided to stay in town, Eddie had vacated his apartment and they decided to make the two-bedroom house a temporary residence.

It was a sweet little house, made all that much prettier thanks to Margo's astute eye. With the permission of the owner—an older couple who lived year-round in Florida now and had no interest in moving back—Margo had painted the walls a soft but warm grey and added curtains to the windows for a touch of color. She'd replaced some of the furniture that came with the house with her own pieces. The result was a tiny jewel box, and a reminder that a beautiful home could be made of even the smallest of spaces.

Bridget made a mental note to ask Margo to give her thoughts on Bridget's living quarters. Although she still used the majority of the downstairs as her own home, the living room and two bedrooms that she and Emma shared could use some sprucing up.

Yes, she'd work on that. It would keep her busy. Her

mind from wandering.

And the wedding! Good grief. Of course she had to think about the wedding.

With that, she opened her car door, then retrieved the wedding gown from the backseat, where she'd laid it carefully.

Margo had promised her that Eddie would not be home today. He was on duty, having taken yesterday off. Still, Bridget felt anxious openly displaying the wedding gown. Margo and Eddie had already had their share of bad luck, which had broken them apart when they were far too young. Now, when they had finally reunited, she didn't dare let anything stand in the way of their happy ending. Even a bit of superstition.

Margo opened the door before Bridget had a chance to knock, which was fortunate, because her arms were full and the dress was so long, even if she were to hold the hanger over her head, she feared the train would skim the ground.

"Oh, look at it!" Margo's hands flew to her mouth.

"It is pretty," Bridget agreed. She felt a twinge of regret, and not for the first time, that her own wedding dress had been a white sundress she'd bought off the sale rack two days before she and Ryan had eloped. No veil. No train. Her bouquet had been pink carnations. Pretty, but not exactly traditional.

"It's more than pretty!" Margo carefully took the dress from Bridget's arms and they both walked into the house.

Immediately Bridget noticed the fresh flowers on the coffee table in the living room, and the new throw pillows too. Light blue this time, rather than the deep red Margo had put out over the holidays.

Why hadn't she thought of something as simple as this?

Spring had arrived and soon it would be summer. She'd lighten up the lobby. Maybe her bedroom, too.

Not that any of the guests saw that. Especially the guest in Room Four.

Ugh. It was official. She had it bad.

"Try it on," she said urgently, and not because she had to pick up Emma in half an hour. She was still nervous that at any moment Eddie might come home. If the inn hadn't been full, she would have insisted that Margo try it on there. "And you promise me you're going to let me bring it home until the big day?"

Margo rolled her eyes good-naturedly. "Don't tell me you believe in that nonsense!"

"Why shouldn't I?" Bridget remarked, sinking into the couch and letting her entire body relax.

"You read too many of those romance novels," Margo tutted as she took the dress upstairs.

Maybe it was true. Maybe Bridget did read too many romance novels. Though, come to think of it, she hadn't had time to read any—not even her newest J.R. Anderson—since Jack had come to the inn…

Well, something to keep her busy when he was gone, then, she thought, drawing no comfort at all from the thought. All too soon Jack would be gone, and that excitement—and hope—would be gone. It would be her again. Just her. And Emma. And the guests.

Suddenly, even though this was all she could have asked for not so long ago, her life had never felt emptier.

"Okay, here I come!" Margo cried from the top of the stairs.

Shaking herself from her thoughts, Bridget turned so she was facing the stairs. "Don't trip!" she warned, imagining the thought. The ripped dress. The twisted ankle.

"Did anyone ever tell you that you worry too much?" Margo said, appearing in the gown that, sure enough, fit her perfectly. "Button me up."

"Oh, Margo." Bridget couldn't help it. She felt her eyes well with tears. "I wish Mom and Dad could see you."

Margo squeezed her hand, tightly. "I know. But I like to think that somewhere, up there, they're watching. And they know. It's one of the reasons I wanted to get married in that house. It wasn't just that we talked about it as children. It's because that house was theirs, ours, full of so many happy memories. It's the closest thing we have to having them with us."

Bridget nodded, struggling to swallow the lump that had formed in her throat. "It's one of the reasons I needed to hold onto the house, too," she said. Suddenly, all her worries about weather and tents and tables disappeared. Margo didn't care about any of that. Not really. And she shouldn't either. They had the house. They had each other.

"This is going to be a beautiful wedding," she promised her sister.

Margo dropped her hand and turned to look at herself in the mirror she'd hung over an accent table. Only Margo would have thought to do this, and it opened the small space, letting in more light from the big windows that looked out onto the ocean.

"I know this sounds weird, but this wedding...it feels different." Margo looked down at the dress, admiring it.

"That's because you're marrying your true love," Bridget said as she slid the first satin-covered button through its hole. She didn't care if that came out like a line from of one of the books her sisters were so keen to tease her about. Margo was marrying her true love. She'd fallen in love with Eddie when she was just a girl, and circumstances had torn them apart, and now, after all these years, when hope had felt loss and experiences had been had, they had grown and changed, and found each other again.

If that wasn't a perfect second chance, she didn't know what was.

Bridget wondered if she'd ever have the chance to say the same for herself some day. And, in a fit of optimism, realized that she just might...

*

An hour later, with Emma in tow, Bridget arrived at Serenity Hills, where Abby already had the search for Pudgie underway. Or so Bridget thought.

When she arrived at Mimi's door, she saw Mimi and Abby watching a black and white movie while simultaneously eating a box of chocolate-covered cherries.

"Yummy!" Emma exclaimed, her eyes lighting up. She looked up at Bridget eagerly. "Can I have one, Mommy!"

"Of course you can," Abby answered for her, and Bridget bit back a wave of irritation. Her sister gave her a suggestive look. "Mimi received these from a secret admirer. They were just sitting on her doormat!"

Bridget frowned. "And you ate them?" She put a hand on Emma's shoulder to stop her from reaching for the box.

Abby's laughter was loud. "Of course we ate them," she said, shaking her head. She plucked another candy from the box and popped it into her mouth. "You really need some spontaneity, Bridget."

Oh, if only Abby knew just how spontaneous she'd been lately, Bridget thought.

"Fine, go ahead and have one, Emma," she said, against her better judgment.

Abby let Emma select a chocolate and then proffered the box toward Bridget. Bridget hesitated and then thought, Why not? She grinned as she sat down and took a bite. "That is good," she admitted.

"I hope they leave another box tomorrow," Mimi remarked.

"Any idea who it was?" Bridget asked.

Mimi shrugged, but Abby said, "I have a hunch. What about that sweet man with the bow tie from the festival? He was rather handsome."

"So you like them older, do you now? I thought you had your eye on that male nurse!" Mimi said, and Bridget couldn't help but be pleased that her grandmother's memory was so sharp today. Indeed, just last fall, Abby had developed a crush on a nurse that worked at Serenity Hills, prompting daily visits for several weeks.

"Oh." Abby pouted. "I had my eye on him. But he had his eye on the girl at the front desk." She took another candy from the box.

"There will be someone else," Bridget assured her, knowing that with Abby, her eye never committed for long.

Abby licked the chocolate from her fingers and gave a casual shrug. "And if there isn't, that's okay. After all, I have my new job to keep me busy. And of course, Margo's wedding to cater!"

Oh, Jesus. Just when Bridget was starting to relax, she felt her stomach knot.

She should have talked to Margo about her concerns when she visited her today. She'd meant to. But it was such a happy time, seeing Margo in the dress, that she didn't want to take away from it.

She'd talk to her. And soon. At the very least, a backup

plan was needed, but how they would find one at this late date, she wasn't sure.

"Everything okay, Bridget?" Abby was looking at her, as were Emma and Mimi.

"Oh, I'm just tired," she said, which wasn't exactly untrue. "It's been busy with a full house this weekend."

"Yes, how many should I plan on for breakfast for tomorrow?" Abby asked, sitting up a little straighter.

"Just one guest," Bridget said. "I don't have any other couples checking in until Saturday."

When Jack checked out, she thought, with a sinking heart.

Really, there was no reason for Abby to come. Not for one guest. She opened her mouth to say just that when she suddenly thought the better of it. Jack had almost kissed her yesterday. And that wasn't a good thing, not if he was leaving in less than a week.

A chaperone was needed. And Abby would be good at that.

Yes, Abby wanted to be put to use. And that she would be. With Abby underfoot, Bridget would be forced to stay professional and not let any feelings get in the way of a clear head.

After all, when Abby was around, someone had to be the adult. And that was usually Bridget.

Chapter Fourteen

By the time Bridget returned from school drop-off on Monday morning, she had to bite her tongue from telling Abby, "I told you so."

"There's no one to serve," she said, gesturing to the bowl of pancake batter that was sitting in front of Abby.

"Maybe," said Abby, with a little lilt in her voice, "you should offer your guest a little room service."

Bridget felt her pulse skip. If Abby had any clue what had already transpired between Bridget and Jack, no doubt her word choice would have a different insinuation. But in this case, her sister had one thing in mind: serving food.

"He's in town to work," Bridget informed her. "I don't want to interrupt him."

"You wouldn't be interrupting him," Abby said

pointedly. "You'd be serving him. The man is probably hungry. Thirsty. He's staying in an inn that doesn't offer room service when he doesn't want to leave his room!"

Abby did make a good point. And it was tempting to think about seeing Jack again. But there was a little part of Bridget that wondered if he'd stayed in his room since Saturday night because he was avoiding her. And what almost happened between them.

Nonsense! She was giving herself far too much credit. He had not kissed her. This time. So really, there was nothing to even think about.

"I'm sure he's left to eat in town," she said to her sister. She came and went throughout the day, and probably hadn't noticed when Jack popped in and out.

Even if she'd looked. A few times. As a concerned innkeeper, of course.

"Well, it's nine thirty and I have these amazing strawberries and cream pancakes I'd love to serve, not to mention that box of pastries that is going to go stale." Here, Abby pinched her lips and made a stern glance at the white bakery box from Angie's Café. "You should at least let him know what his options are."

Bridget hesitated. All her guests knew what time breakfast hours were. It was written on the information card she kept on the bedside table. She assumed that Jack still had his. Not that she could be certain of this. Unlike the other guests, who happily allowed her entrance to make their beds and refresh their sheets, Jack's door handle permanently boasted the Do Not Disturb sign.

"Well, if you're not going to do it, I'll do it myself!" Abby announced.

Bridget popped off the counter stool. "No...I'll go. You're right," she said, trying to convince herself of that. "He's probably hungry and I should at least offer something to his room, considering he's our only guest."

If this were a woman, say in her fifties, with the same workload and same need for privacy, would she extend an offer of breakfast being delivered to her room?

Yes.

And that was her answer.

He wasn't Jack Riley. Jack with the nut-brown tousled hair and warm eyes and oh so kissable lips.

He was a guest. And so help her, he would be treated as one.

She walked through the dining room with growing dread, wishing that he might just appear at any moment instead, and spare her from interrupting him. But when she rounded the corner to the front hall, there was no one there, and so she took each step slowly, moving as quietly as she could up the stairs until she was standing directly in front of the white-painted door with a single oil-rubbed bronze number hanging from it.

The DO NOT DISTURB sign hung firmly from the knob, just as it had last evening, when she'd come home from Serenity Hills and, after settling Emma into her room to have a tea party with her dolls, made the rounds to change the bedding after her weekend guests had checked out.

She strained for any sounds in the room, heat creeping up her cheeks when she considered the possibility that the man could still be sleeping. After all, it was entirely possible that he'd worked all through the night and had only just now fallen asleep and—

He is a fifty-six-year-old woman with a wart on her nose and three grandchildren. He is not a handsome, single man of a respectable age. He is hungry. He is your guest.

She knocked.

Oh, Jesus. Her heart began to pound as she stood and waited, waited for a door in her own house to fling open. The door that had once opened into a purple and pink bedroom complete with celebrity fan posters and a shocking amount of nail polish bottles that Abby arranged by color.

She waited, and just when she began to calm down and conclude that he was not going to open the door, he did.

*

Jack wasn't one to lie. Not even to himself. When he heard the knock on the door, he considered not answering it. He was in the midst of a thought, a good one, one he might lose if he stepped away from the keyboard, even for a minute.

But now, looking at Bridget, in her pale pink T-shirt and bright blue eyes, he was glad he had.

"Am I disturbing you?" she asked.

"I was just about to take a break," he said, even though this wasn't true at all.

Her shoulders seemed to relax. "I just wanted to let you know that breakfast is ready. Can I invite you down to the dining room, or would you prefer a tray in your room?"

So that's all it was then? Formal hospitality. He couldn't help but feel a bit of disappointment that the reason for her visit wasn't a bit more…personal. Something had shifted between them in the past week, and, despite how hard he was fighting it, something was changing in him, too. It was showing, in his writing. A passion and an interest that hadn't been there in a long time.

"I should probably stay in and work today," he admitted. God knew if he went downstairs, he might never get back to his room again today, and he still had a job to do.

"Of course, of course." Bridget nodded, but there was a sense of disappointment in her expression that he felt too. "I can bring you up dinner tonight. It's no trouble."

The thought of eating meal after meal, alone in his room, when he could be downstairs, or out, exploring this town, left him feeling nothing short of depressed. He didn't know what to make of that. He had come here to do exactly that, after all. And now…now it was the last thing he wanted to do. And not because he wanted to avoid writing.

Because he finally wanted to stop avoiding living.

"Do you ever let guests use your kitchen?" he asked suddenly.

Bridget shrugged, seeming surprised by the question. "I've never had the request before, but I'm sure that can be arranged. Why?"

"How about dinner tonight?" he suggested, before rational thought could take over, put him in check, remind him what a truly stupid idea this was. "On me?"

She laughed. "You mean, I'd be the guest? In my own home?"

"That's right," he said. When she put it that way, it was kind of a nice thought. And he'd like to do something nice for her. He had the impression that not enough people did. "I'll even do the shopping. I should probably get some fresh air at some point today, after all."

"You're really working hard in here, aren't you?"

"I am," he confessed. "I haven't felt this good in a long time, actually. And I have you to thank."

"Me?" She flushed a little.

He nodded. "Being here, around you, it's…opened my eyes. Cleared my head. Let me return the favor by doing something nice for you," he said.

She looked so pleased, he knew he had made the right call. "Well, all right then. Name your time."

"Would eight be too late?'

"Emma goes to bed at eight," Bridget said, looking at him carefully. "I think eight would be perfect."

*

"So?" Abby asked when Bridget appeared in the kitchen a moment later, grinning ear to ear and wishing she had more control on her emotions.

"So…what?" Bridget asked.

Abby's eyes widened. "Is he having breakfast?"

Oh, that. Bridget nodded. "Yes. Yes, he'll have breakfast."

Abby pursed her lips as she flicked on the burner on the range. "I must say, Bridget, I've never seen you quite so flustered when it came to a guest before."

Bridget picked up her coffee mug and took a long sip. It sobered her. Cleared her head. Pushed out all those silly little notions that were already getting her into trouble with her sister.

"You've only been around the inn for a week," she pointed out.

Abby shrugged. "True." But she didn't look convinced.

"Is this the man with the thick brown hair and the nice eyes? From New York, right? The one who came with you to the festival?"

Bridget didn't know where her sister was going with this, but she didn't like it, either. "Yes. Why?"

"Just asking." Abby's grin was cheeky. She waited until after she'd added the batter to the pan, in perfect, symmetrical circles, Bridget was rather impressed to notice, before saying, "He's single."

Bridget felt her face heat, and she didn't need a mirror to tell her it was red. She busied herself with fetching a tray, even though the job could have been done in three seconds flat, considering the drawer was at her feet. "Is he?" God, she was a bad liar. She should have just said, "I know." Because she did know, of course she did, and Abby knew it!

This was the same tactic that Abby used to use when she was trying to get Bridget to confess that she knew where their parents had hidden the Christmas gifts, once she had stopped believing in Santa, that was.

"He is," Abby said.

Silence lingered. Bridget knew she should let it go, Abby was just trying to yank her chain, get a reaction. But why?

Abby began to hum, a rather annoying tune, and loudly, obviously, until finally Bridget couldn't take it anymore.

"Why do you ask?" She was mad at herself for feeding into it the moment the words were out of her mouth.

"Oh, no reason." Abby's eyes glimmered when she turned back to the island where she sprinkled a bowl of strawberries with sugar.

No reason indeed, Bridget thought.

Chapter Fifteen

Jack drove into town, realizing only once he'd gotten to the center of the four-square blocks that comprised Oyster Bay, that he hadn't even had to check the route this time. Landmarks were becoming about as familiar as the people here, and despite not being able to blend into the crowd as he usually preferred, he liked that.

He parked across the street from the bookstore, recalling the food market he'd spotted across the street on that first morning he'd walked through town.

What a difference a week made, he thought, as he slipped four quarters into the meter and, grabbing a basket, entered the store.

A week ago he'd been stressed and anxious, and now he was shopping for ingredients for dinner…for a woman. He almost laughed out loud at the mere thought of it.

Knowing from the lasagna dinner Bridget made that she liked Italian food, he decided on a simple pasta that even a bad cook like himself couldn't mess up, too bad, and a fresh pesto sauce. A good bottle of wine and something with chocolate would round out the meal, not that he was exactly sure what would happen after dessert.

He knew what he wanted to happen. He wanted to kiss her. Again. Just like he'd wanted to on Saturday, after the festival. And this time, if she let him, he would.

He wouldn't over think it, or dwell on the past. He'd lived there too long, and now, being in the present, he actually dared to look at the future for the first time in too long.

His phone rang, and he glanced at the screen, pulling him out of this town and back to his life in New York all at once. He considered not answering it, but knew there was no dodging it anymore.

"Lance!" His agent of twelve years and friend for just as many used to be someone he looked forward to hearing from, until everything started to unravel. Then his calls became the source of tension, and pressure, and often he tried to avoid them as much as possible.

"You sound suspiciously happy to hear from me," Lance replied in that gruff voice of his.

Jack stopped in front of the wine aisle, feeling guilty. He'd turned his back on more than just himself in recent years. He'd shut out the world. But he'd always shut out people who still cared about him.

"I take it that means you're making progress?" Lance asked, almost nervously.

Here, Jack grinned. "I'm happy to inform you that, yes, I have had a breakthrough."

Lance whistled under his breath. "How'd it happen?"

Jack opened his mouth to start to explain and then, because he couldn't help himself, he said, "I guess it's sometimes just as simple as boy meets girl."

"So you stopped over thinking things!" Lance said, and Jack could hear the smile in his voice. "I knew a change of scenery would do you good."

"You were right," he said. As always. After all, wasn't it Lance who told him to slow down, take Erin on a vacation, live his life so he'd have experiences to tell?

"When are you going to figure out that I'm always right?" Lance joked.

The conversation was coming to a close, but Jack had one more thing he needed to say first. "Let's grab dinner when I get back. Like old times," he added, hoping that Lance would still be up for that sort of thing. Lately all their interactions had resorted to business talk. Slowly, without even noticing, over time their friendship had faded into a professional relationship only.

"I'd like that," Lance said.

"Met too," Jack said, and disconnected the call.

The familiar sense of anxiety that had followed him around for years started to rear, but he pushed it aside as quickly as it appeared. Enough. He had lived that way for too long. And that hadn't been living at all, had it? He'd been getting up, eating, going to bed, but that was no life. Here, in his brief stay in Oyster Bay, he had dared to live.

One day at a time, he told himself. He'd enjoy today. He wouldn't let worrying about tomorrow ruin it.

And maybe, he thought, when he pictured Bridget's sweet smile and that easy way she drew him out of himself, he wouldn't have to worry anymore.

*

The day after a big weekend was always the busiest, Bridget had found. Sometimes, it felt even busier than the day the guests all checked in. Now there were rooms to clean and beds to change. Vacuuming. Laundry. Inevitably something always spilled and needed to be cleaned up. Once, a shower curtain had been ripped. Another time a perfume bottle had broken and the entire upstairs had to be fumigated, with the windows up, even though it was February and freezing and the heating bill had skyrocketed. Bridget had lived with a five-day low-grade headache, but by the weekend, when guests checked in again, the air was clear and nothing was amiss.

Still, ever since, Bridget got twitchy when she noticed a guest wearing cologne.

But today, for the first time since perhaps her first month since opening the inn, when the novelty of having actual guests had worn off, she didn't mind the laborious chores. In fact, she was happy to have them. They easily passed the time between now and...dinner.

Her stomach rumbled just at the thought and she had to force herself to focus on the task at hand, which was laundering the towels and making sure that she didn't accidentally slip in a red sock. Pink guest towels didn't fit the design of the house, which was light and airy with shades of blues, teals, and greens.

She started the load and checked her watch, pleased and nervous all at once to see that it was already two o'clock. She hadn't even stopped to eat lunch, she'd been so busy going room by room, all six guest rooms except Room Four, of course. When she'd been upstairs earlier, the DO NOT DISTURB sign was hanging from the knob and she could hear the faint tapping of fingers on a keyboard through the wall.

Normally, she would be hurrying to finish up this latest round before she had to go pick up Emma, but an hour ago Ryan had called and offered to take her to that movie. Monday nights were his easy nights, when people were tired and broke from the weekend and eager to eat in, not hang out in the pub. Any other time, Bridget would have pointed out that it was a school night, not a good time to be out late for a movie, but not tonight.

Tonight was, in fact, a perfect night for Ryan to have Emma. And Emma would surely be excited to sleep in that tent again...on a school night.

A tent. Bridget could only shake her head.

Bridget finished folding the load of towels she had just pulled from the dryer and carried the basket down the hall and up the stairs. When they were stacked in the linen cabinet just outside Room Two, she paused and wondered if she could run the vacuum or if the noise would distract Jack. She chewed her lip, at war with two sides of hospitality, and was just about to go to the closet where she kept the vacuum when she saw that, for the first time since Jack had checked in last weekend, there was no sign hanging from his door.

Now, this was strange...

She walked over to his door, checked the floor, searching to see if it might have slipped off. Frowning, she stood completely still and listened for any sound that might be coming from the room, but the typing had stopped.

Did he want her to clean the room? That would make sense, if it hadn't been for the fact that he seemed so determined not to have any service until now.

She tapped on the door, and waited.

No response. He must have gone to the store, she realized, as another swell of nerves ripped through her stomach. Really, this had to stop. She was acting like a teenage girl about to go to prom!

But oh, it was nice to feel like a teenager again, she thought with a grin,

Fishing her keys from her pocket, she turned the locked and let herself into the room.

Or...the mess.

She stared, not blinking, at the room. It was east facing

with a view of the lawn and the ocean beyond, and painted a soft teal blue. It was, without a doubt, one of her favorite rooms in the house, even more so than Room Three, which had been her bedroom growing up.

Margo and she had decided to give this particular room all white furniture, with a pale blue and white print duvet cover. They'd put a desk under the window, framed by heavy drapes, and added glass lamp bases to the bedside tables.

But you couldn't see those lamp bases now. Or the desk. At least not its surface. It was too littered with papers and paper cups and pens. And as for the beautiful duvet cover…half of it was on the floor, and the pillows on the bed were all bunched up. In fact, if she looked close enough, she could almost make out the imprint of Jack's head!

The curtains were open, but the blinds were drawn, and the room felt dark, when it was meant to be light and airy.

In all the months that Bridget had run the Harper House Inn, she had never seen a room in such a state. Had it been any other guest, she probably would have cried. But because it was Jack, she laughed. She laughed and laughed until she had to stifle the sound with her own fist, just in case he came back from the store and heard her.

Well. This was certainly a task that would keep her busy up until her date—make that dinner—tonight.

She started with the bed, stripping it, tugging fresh

sheets into place—with hospital corners—and fluffing the pillows. She spread the duvet over the mattress, trying not to think that in a matter of hours, Jack would climb into this bed and...

No. No more thinking that way. Really, she didn't like to think about what any of the guests did in these bedrooms. It was too weird.

She moved onto the bathroom, where towels were on the floor or barely hanging from their hooks and gathered them up into her arms, resisting the urge to take a sniff.

Okay, so maybe she didn't completely resist. Maybe, just maybe, right before she dumped them into the laundry basket that had just held fresh, folded towels, she took a discreet...breath.

Musk. Woods. Man.

Oh, Bridget.

She dropped them into the basket and turned to look at the room. It was so much better, she could only begin to imagine what Jack would think when he returned. Would he be embarrassed, or relieved?

She just wouldn't mention this. Maybe she'd pretend she had a maid who came in. Spare them an awkward moment in what should be an otherwise...special evening.

The man was stressed, after all. And he was on vacation. Maybe he had been waiting for service every day, and that service had never come, because of the sign, and maybe he hadn't even realized that there was a sign, and...

Oh, here she went. Making excuses again. The man was a slob. There. If that was his worst quality, she'd take it.

She was just turning to go when she eyed the desk. She chewed her lip, not wanting to pry, but curious all the same. At the floor was a waste paper basket, overflowing.

Of course! She still had to empty the baskets! She gathered the one in the bathroom first and then, more slowly, walked toward the desk. She didn't open any notebooks, or light up his computer, tempting as it was. She simply bent down, picked up the trash can and saw something that made her promptly drop it.

"What?" she said aloud. Her heart began to hammer in her chest and she suddenly didn't even remember that she was standing here, in a guest's room, staring at his personal belongings.

The notebook was open, the first page filled, from top to bottom, overwriting every margin, and squeezing in words between spaces, but one thing was crystal clear. The name. The series name. Her series. Her favorite series. The series that had given her comfort and joy and hope.

Jack Riley. J.R. But...it couldn't be.

She looked down, peering closer at the words that were scribbled on the page. The characters' names were familiar; names she had come to know, their stories ones she had anticipated. And here it was. The next book, unfolding before her in her very guest room. Only the story was familiar for another reason too. A bookstore. A wedding. A kiss. An innkeeper.

Bridget stepped away from the desk, her mouth completely dry.

None of this made any sense, but wasn't that how life went? Things were what they were, and sometimes you chose to believe them or sometimes you tried to make them fit what you wanted them to be.

And no matter how much she could hope that this wasn't what she thought it was, it was. Jack was J.R. Anderson. And she was his material.

Nothing more.

*

Bridget was waiting in the kitchen when the front door opened an hour later, and there was Jack, two bags from The Corner Market in his hands, a cheerful grin on his face.

It slipped the moment he saw her. "Something wrong?"

"I cleaned your room," she said, and immediately his eyes went round.

"Oh, God. Oh. You know, wow. I usually don't live like that, but this deadline was getting to me and I wasn't coming out of the room much and..."

She pulled in a breath. It wasn't the messy room. It was so much more.

"I saw the notes to your new book, Jack," she said.

"Or should I say, Mr. Anderson?"

He closed his eyes, his jaw setting as he set the bags on the counter. "Look, I can explain."

"Explain what part?" Bridget cried. "That you listened to me go on and on about how much I love your books and you didn't think to mention to me that you are the author?"

"I use a pen name for a reason," he said.

"This isn't the same," Bridget said, holding firm. She willed herself to stay strong, to get out before she fell in. To spare herself the way she hadn't before. It was always excuse after excuse with Ryan, and she'd listened, because it was easier that way. And look how that had turned out.

"It's not the same, but it is. I'm Jack. J.R. Anderson is...my career." He pulled in a breath, stared at her as if he was debating whether or not to say something. "It's been a long time since I've felt like the author of those books."

She thought of what he'd told her about the writer's block, part of her wanting to sympathize with him as much as the other part wanted to punish him. He'd lied to her. Listened to her go on and on! "You could have told me. Hell, I was your number one fan."

He frowned at her use of the past tense.

"Bridget, listen to me, please. It's been a really long time since I spent time with anyone, or opened up to anyone. I didn't want you to know me as the person behind those books. I wanted you to know me as me."

She folded her arms across her chest, willing herself

not to feed into the flattery, the words that would have otherwise made her heart swell and fill her with a sense of possibility.

"Why were you getting to know me, Jack?" She swallowed the emotion in her voice, but it was there, she couldn't hide it.

"Because I like you!" he exclaimed.

"You do, huh?" She shook her head. "You like the bookstore meeting and the kiss at the wedding you crashed. Maybe you even really did like that Flower Fest…if it made for a good scene in your book."

His eyes flashed. "Bridget."

"You used me, Jack," Bridget said, all emotion and hurt now gone from her steely voice. "You led me on, you used me, and now…" Now, he'd broken her heart.

And stolen from her. Stolen all those stories that had brightened her dark days. They were all a joke. Fantasy.

"I think you should leave," she said, turning away from him. She couldn't look at that face, at those eyes, not for another second.

He was still there, in the room, she could sense him behind her. But he didn't say a word. She stood, staring out onto the water, where she imagined her own wedding someday, back when she was just a little girl like Emma, and her entire world felt so full of wonder.

But it was just a yard, and the sand, and the ocean. Nothing more.

And those dreams…would never come true. And

shame on her for ever thinking they would.

Her eyes were hot with tears, preventing her from turning around even if she wanted to, and a part of her did. A part of her wanted this to be made right. To find an explanation that was somehow enough.

"I didn't use you, Bridget," Jack said softly.

And then...he was gone.

.

Chapter Sixteen

The first thing Bridget saw when she woke up the next morning was the name J.R. Anderson, in its familiar block letters, gracing the spine of the paperback that had sat on her bedside table since she first bought it in Trish's store.

She groaned and closed her eyes, wishing yesterday had been a bad dream and knowing, from the weight in her chest, that it was not. Jack was gone. And maybe, in a way, he had never really been here at all.

Two weeks ago, life had been good. Solid. Busy. She had wanted for nothing, really. But one week ago, life had felt so full of excitement, and promise, and hope.

And today…today life felt different. Bleak in a way. Like she had lost something, even if it had been just as fictional as the book sitting beside her.

She reached for it, held it in her hands. But instead of

flinging it across the room like a part of her wanted to, or gathering it up with all the others she had enjoyed so much over the years and dumping them in the trash, she instead stared at the cover and then, after a moment, cracked the spine.

She ran a hand over the paper, her eyes skimming the first chapter. Every word on this page had been written by Jack. How was this possible? Jack who didn't believe in love, had written all of these words that had touched her so deeply and made her believe again?

She thought of the look in his eyes when she'd called him out, forced him to be honest with her. There was hurt there, and not because she'd uncovered the truth.

Or maybe that was just what she wanted to see. She was good at that, after all. She'd gone through it with Ryan. Tried to fit him in a box, make him the man she wanted him to be, not the person he really was.

And Jack…Jack had told her who he was from the start. A man who didn't believe in the product he was selling. A man who was blocked and desperate. A man who had used her.

She thought again of what he'd said. That he hadn't used her. That she'd inspired him.

But it didn't change anything, did it?

She closed her eyes again, tossing the book aside. These books didn't matter anymore, and maybe they never should have. They were fairytales, and life wasn't a fairy tale. And they were fantasy.

Fantasy. Just like he had told her.

*

Abby let herself in the kitchen door of the inn, ten minutes late, and bracing herself for a lecture from Bridget on the merits of punctuality. But Bridget wasn't at the kitchen island this morning. She wasn't in the kitchen at all. The lights were off and the house was eerily quiet.

Frowning, Abby closed the door behind her and stood perfectly still, wondering if her clocks were wrong and she was somehow even later than she'd feared. Or earlier?

But no, the clock above the range proved that she was, in fact, only ten minutes late. Still, it was nearly eight o'clock. Shouldn't Bridget be frantically getting Emma ready for school while attending to the guests?

Her blood ran cold when she considered that something had happened to her sister. That a guest had turned homicidal, maybe done her in. Or kidnapped her. Anything was possible, after all.

Right, she was going in.

With a sharp knock on the door to Bridget's quarters, she stood and waited with a pounding heart, and her pulse didn't settle until a few minutes later, when the door swung open and Bridget stood there, still in pajamas, her hair a mess, her eyes red and puffy.

Of course! She hadn't even considered the more logical possibility that Bridget was sick.

"Oh, no. Are you not feeling well?" Abby all but licked her lips. If Bridget wasn't feeling well, then maybe Abby could use this opportunity to show her that she could be relied on to take over in a pinch. She could braid Emma's hair, take her to school, and whip up a delicious breakfast for the guests. She might even be willing to freshen the linens and do a little light housekeeping. My, wouldn't Bridget be impressed then. She had it in her; Bridget just didn't know it yet. For some reason…

"I didn't sleep well last night," was all Bridget said. Of course. Tight-lipped Bridget. Even if she was sick or feverish, she wouldn't show weakness.

Abby bit back a wave of frustration and decided to point out the obvious. "Well, you don't look well at all. Do you need me to get Emma ready for school?"

"Emma spent the night at Ryan's," Bridget replied.

Huh. Well that was…unusual. Bridget never sent Emma to her father's unless it was a scheduled day.

Well, there was the evidence then. Bridget might not be willing to admit it to her own sister, but clearly she had admitted it to herself. She was sick. And she needed help. And Abby was the girl for the job.

"Well, you clearly need more rest. Go back to bed and leave the guests to me."

"There are no guests," Bridget replied, and put a hand to her forehead. "Damn it. I meant to call you and I forgot."

Bridget? Admitting she wasn't perfect? Something was very wrong indeed.

"No guests?" Abby said. "But I thought Room Four was staying through the week?"

She stopped, as it all became far too clear. Of course.

Jack had checked out early. And Bridget was...heartbroken.

She gave her sister a sympathetic smile and said, "This sounds like the perfect opportunity for us to have a nice breakfast together then. I'll get the coffee started."

"You don't have to—" Bridget protested.

"I want to," Abby stressed. "You're always taking care of all of us. Let me do something nice for you for once."

Bridget's smile was so grateful that it made Abby feel like crying. Oh, Bridget. Why did she always have to make life so much harder for herself than she needed to? Why didn't she see that Abby had been right here, all along, happy to help. Eager to be...wanted.

She started the coffee while Bridget sank into a counter stool, then went to the island to start the breakfast. Today she'd planned on making a quiche, but the emotional climate called for comfort food. Bread pudding it was.

"So..." she said, as she quickly stirred the mixture and added it to a baking dish. "You want to talk about it?"

"Nothing to talk about," Bridget said with a shrug.

For once, Abby wasn't going to take this evasion. Once in a while, when things were really bad, she managed to get Bridget to open up. Today was going to be one of those days.

"You liked him," Abby said.

"He wasn't who I thought he was," Bridget replied.

"Really?" Abby frowned as she slid the dish into the

preheated oven. "How so?"

"He…wasn't truthful with me. He hid things about himself from me," she said.

"Maybe he just wasn't ready to share yet." Abby tipped her head. "Maybe he was guarded. That's not a terrible thing, after all."

No, Bridget supposed, it wasn't. "The thing is that up until he came, I was happy," Bridget said.

Abby looked her sister in the eye, realizing for the first time that this was true. All this time she'd wanted her sister to get married, settle down again, find someone to ease the list of responsibilities she seemed determined to complain about at every turn. But really, Bridget liked that life. She liked being busy. She liked being, well, needed.

"You still have the inn. And Emma. And Mimi. And me," Abby laughed, but Bridget's smile was wan. Abby frowned and took her sister's hand. "But something's missing?"

"Maybe it always was? Maybe I never stopped wanting what I hoped for in the first place." Bridget shrugged. "I wanted a family. A real, traditional life like we had. I wanted that for Emma. And…I wanted it for myself, I guess."

"Ryan was never the man for that job," Abby said, knowing that Bridget wouldn't argue.

"Neither was Jack."

"No," Abby agreed. "I suppose not. But…maybe one good thing came from his visit?"

Bridget's eyes were hooded. "What's that?" she asked

flatly.

"He made you look inside yourself again. He pulled you out of those books—"

"His books!" Bridget cried. "His stories!"

"So he gave you those too. And he also gave you another experience. A real one. A few days to see how it might have been and how it still can be." Abby grinned. "Jack might not have been the guy for you in the long run, but he made you see that it can still happen."

Bridget nodded, albeit a little begrudgingly. "Since when did you become so wise?"

"I've been this way all along. You just never saw it," Abby said, feeling the sting of hurt at the truth in those words.

Bridget looked at her. "I'm sorry, Abby. I guess to me, you'll always be my silly little sister."

Silly little sister. Abby knew that Bridget hadn't intended to hurt her, but it did all the same. "I'm not so little anymore," she said. "Or silly."

"No," Bridget said. "I suppose you're not."

"And I know you think you need to protect me or take care of me, but believe it or not, I've been doing just fine on my own. Even if it's not the way you would do things, it suits me."

Bridget took a moment to take this in. "I suppose I never looked at that way. I guess I've been waiting for you to settle down…"

"Everyone settles down in their own way. Margo

found her happy ending with Eddie. But me? I found mine with this." Abby grinned, and then, because she just couldn't help it, she flung her arms around Bridget's neck. "Thanks, Bridget."

"For what?" Bridget blinked in surprise.

"For taking a chance on me. I know I don't have the best track record...but I just needed, well, a chance."

Bridget smiled. "We all do, honey. We all do."

*

Another box of chocolates had arrived from Mimi's admirer when Bridget and Abby stopped by later that day, with Emma in tow. The women polished off the box while speculating its source, but Bridget had to admit that even a fine European chocolate couldn't ease the tug in her chest.

"Why don't we take a walk?" she suggested. "A little fresh air is always nice. Mimi, we could go sit in the garden. See what new flowers have sprung." She needed to clear her head, keep moving. Moving forward, she thought. Once she'd mastered it. She'd had no choice. But doing it the second time around felt like more of a challenge somehow.

Mimi didn't seem thrilled by the idea, but she didn't complain either. With that, the four girls tossed the empty box of chocolates and pushed Mimi out into the hallway. Normally, they took the same path to the building's courtyard, but today Bridget wanted to try another route. Mimi needed all the variety she could get.

They were only halfway down a corridor Bridget had never tried despite the fact that they all pretty much looked the same with their wood doors and floral wallpaper, when Abby slowed her pace.

"Do you hear a noise?" she asked, frowning.

"What kind of a noise?" she asked, pushing Mimi toward the corner, but Abby grabbed her hand, forcing her to stop.

"I mean it. Listen. It's…" They stood in silence for a moment before Abby turned to Bridget and mouthed, "I think it's Pudgie."

Bridget's eyes grew wide as she strained to hear. There was the muffled sound of television that could always be heard through the doors, a woman's voice down the hall, the conversation too hard to make out, and then…the distinct sound of a cat's meow.

Her heart began to race, but she forced it firmly in place. Mimi wasn't the only one with a cat in this building. A few of the residents had fish, too, and the ones who spotted Emma in the hall always invited her to sprinkle a little food into their bowls.

"It could be anything," she said to Abby.

"But you hear it?" Abby wasn't going to let this go. She walked over to the partially open door at the end of the hall, pressed her ear against the wood, and nodded. "I'm going to check it out."

"Are you serious?" Bridget looked down at Mimi who was shaking her head.

"That girl gets more confused every day," she remarked, citing a line that Emma had overheard Margo saying about Mimi one time when the sisters didn't think anyone was in ear shot.

"She'll be right back," Bridget said, bracing herself for Abby's return.

Abby poked her head out of the room a second later, her broad grin telling Bridget everything she needed to know. Relief washed over her, and she couldn't wait to see how Mimi would react to this.

"You have to see this," Abby said, motioning them forward.

Bridget pushed Mimi into the hall, the woman grumbling that Bridget didn't know where she was going, until she saw Pudgie, sitting on the lap of the man they'd seen at the Flower Fest, and then her hand flew to her heart.

"Pudgie!" Mimi's eyes filled with tears, and despite her own reservations toward Pudgie, Bridget's did too.

"Where did you find him?" Bridget asked, grinning at the man who was smiling ear to ear.

"Oh, I didn't find him," he corrected her. "He found me."

Abby frowned. "What do you mean?"

"Pudgie here likes the tuna on crackers that I like to snack on when I watch *Wheel of Fortune* at four."

Bridget exchanged a glance with Abby. "He's been here before today?"

"He's been here for over a week!" The man gave

Pudgie a fond pat on the head, and it was then that Bridget realized just how at home Pudgie seemed in the man's room.

"But...there are signs up for Pudgie's return! All over the building! You couldn't have missed the announcements they've made at dinner. Or breakfast and lunch." Abby was growing red in the face, her green eyes blazing as she stared at the man. "My grandmother's been sick with worry!"

"I never meant to worry her. I just thought...well, if Pudgie liked me, Margaret Harper might too."

"You mean...You've had Pudgie all this time?" Bridget didn't know whether to feel angry or relieved.

"How else was I supposed to get the woman's attention?"

"You kidnapped Pudgie?" Emma's blue eyes were so wide, Bridget could see the whites around them.

"Well, now, young lady, don't go making accusations. I didn't kidnap this little fellow." He patted Pudgie, who did seem quite content on his lap. "He came to visit me. And he decided to stay."

Oh, for God's sake. Bridget looked over at Mimi, who seemed nothing short of bewildered.

"Were you ever going to tell me?" she finally asked.

"Oh, of course! It was never my intent to steal the little guy. I just wanted to get to know you."

Bridget half expected Mimi to tell him where to go with this bold idea, but instead, she patted her lap, and smiled brightly as Pudgie settled himself in. "Well," she said. "You have me here. Now what do you have to say for yourself?"

The man could barely contain his excitement. "It's Bingo night in the community room. Care to join me?"

Mimi demurred only long enough to pat her hair. "I suppose I could. But I'll need to check my calendar first."

Bridget shook her head as she led Emma out of the room, holding her by the hand.

"Are they going to kiss and get married?" Emma asked.

Bridget pulled in a breath. Her grandmother had married at eighteen, and still kept a framed photo of her husband on her nightstand, almost thirty years after his death. She'd been a youngish widow, Bridget realized now, looking back, and in all that time, she'd never dated, never expressed any interest in anyone but her son and his wife, and of course, Bridget and her sisters. And later, Emma.

And now, all these years later, she'd opened her heart. At least for a night of Bingo. Maybe there really was a second chance for everyone.

Or at least, the possibility of one, she thought, thinking of Jack. And J.R. Anderson. And the fact that somewhere, underneath it all, they were the same man.

Chapter Seventeen

It was a beautiful day for a wedding. So beautiful, in fact, that some might call it perfect. The sun was shining and the sky was blue and all of their closest friends and family were gathered in the tent, watching Margo and Eddie take their first dance.

Bridget smiled a little sadly as she watched Eddie give her sister a twirl, eliciting a wave of cheers from the crowd.

She didn't know why she felt the tug in her heart. Maybe it was because her parents weren't here to witness the moment that their middle daughter finally found her happy ending. Or maybe…maybe it was because she couldn't help but wish she'd found hers.

She reached for her champagne glass and took a small sip. Emma was curled up in the chair beside her, her flower girl dress slightly rumpled, and the wreath of pink flowers askew in her hair. She was already falling asleep, no doubt crashing after her two slices of wedding cake.

Yes, the old Bridget would have twitched over this, but today, Bridget didn't have the heart to get anxious over small things, or small joys. Emma enjoyed a carefree night. They both did.

Spontaneity, she decided, could be a good thing, even if it didn't always end the way you hoped. Sometimes life's little surprises were moments of light, and laughter, and happiness, even if they were fleeting.

All the more reason to treasure them, she thought.

Bridget was giving serious consideration to getting a second slice for herself when she felt a tap on her shoulder. She froze, her breath catching as her heart began to pound, wondering, against all rational thought, if it was Jack. If he'd come back, even if she hadn't heard from him since he left the inn more than a week ago, and why should she? She shouldn't even want to, considering...

She turned, oh so slowly, and felt her heart sink a little when she saw her Uncle Chip standing above her, holding out a hand. "Humor me with a dance?"

"Oh, Chip." Bridget smiled. "I'd love to."

She took his arm as they walked to the dance floor, where he led her into a classic box step, reminding her of all the times she'd danced exactly this way with her father, but never at her own wedding. Instead she'd eloped, given up the chance to be walked down the aisle, to have her father give her away...

She felt her eyes mist with regret.

"Everything okay, Bridge?" Chip asked, tipping his head.

"Just...sentimental." Her smile felt watery. "I'm happy for Bridget. I just, well, I can't help wondering where I went so wrong." She paused, wondering if she should ask Chip the one question that had always been on her mind.

"Why didn't you ever remarry, Chip? I mean, you're sweet, funny..."

"And handsome?" He laughed, but there was hurt behind it. He shrugged. "I guess you could say that I didn't need to. I had something perfect, even if it was only for a brief amount of time. And when it was over...Well, it couldn't be replaced."

"She broke your heart," Bridget said, thinking of the way Chip's wife had run off, leaving him with two young girls, all those years ago.

"She stole my heart. Maybe she didn't deserve it, but, well, that's how it is."

"You didn't want to try again?"

"Didn't see a reason to. I had my girls. My restaurant. You lot." He pulled a face that made her laugh. "My life is full."

Bridget nodded slowly. Her life was, too. So full that sometimes she felt she couldn't add one more thing to her list, one more responsibility to her day.

But there was something missing. And she hadn't

realized it until now.

"And you? What's your excuse?"

Bridget laughed. Only Chip could be so blunt, and God she loved him for it. She squeezed him a little tighter, so grateful for his presence in her life. "I have a daughter. And an inn. And Mimi. And my sisters."

"They're all taken care of," Chip said, and Bridget realized that it was true. Somehow things had fallen into place. Margo was married. Mimi had found not just Pudgie, but a new companion. And Abby...had found her passion. And followed her heart.

"Emma will grow, and she will leave."

Bridget scowled at him. "Gee, thanks."

"I'm just saying what's true, and I speak from experience. Look at my two spread out over the country," Chip said. "Just don't shut yourself off to the possibility of a second chance. Promise me that."

Bridget sighed. "You know I can never say no to you."

"Good, because I believe there's someone else who wants to dance with you, and I insist that you take his offer," Chip said, jutting his chin as he released his hold on her.

She looked at him, startled, but all he could do was wink and whisper, "Remember what I said about second chances..."

Bridget's heart was pounding as he backed away, grinning ear to ear, and she was left alone on the dance floor. But not for long.

She turned, hoping it was Jack almost as much as she

didn't dare to hope at all.

And there he was. A champagne flute in each hand. A sheepish grin on his face.

And for not the first time in a long time, Bridget dared to believe again.

*

Well, she hadn't run. Jack took this as good news. Still, she wasn't smiling either. Instead she was looking at him in confusion, or surprise; he couldn't tell.

He pulled in a breath. He'd come here. Taken a chance. Crashed another damn wedding.

It was time to finish the job.

"I didn't realize you were on the guest list," she said, and he appreciated her attempt at lightening the mood. Bridget, ever hospitable, ever sweet...

It was why he'd come back. Why he never should have left in the first place.

"In all fairness, I waited until after dinner was served," he said, grinning, but she didn't return the gesture.

Right. Of course. Why should she? He'd lied to her; by omission, but still. He'd kissed her. More than once. And despite everything he'd said about not believing in romance or love, he'd lied about that too. Because he did. Now.

Thanks to her.

"I know you have no reason to trust me," he said.

"No," she said. "I don't."

Right. Of course. Jack nodded. He could leave. Turn around. But it couldn't end here. Not like this.

"And I know you have no reason to believe me when I say that I do believe in all those things. Romance. Love." He motioned to the bride and groom, gliding across the dance floor.

"Why now? Why suddenly?" she said.

"Because of you," he said honestly. "Because being here, in this house, letting someone in…it felt good, Bridget. And it's been a long time since I've felt that good."

She nodded, slowly. "I understand," she softly. "I…felt the same way."

"And it's scary," he admitted.

"It is," she said, looking up at him, her blue eyes so earnest, that he knew he'd been right to come. To take a chance. To try again.

"I don't want to mess this up," he said. "I don't want…to go back to the way I did all those years ago. I don't want to be disappointed. Or hurt. Or to feel like I somehow failed someone else. And myself."

She took a step back, but that urged him forward. "And I don't want to walk out of here the way I did last week and go back to that empty apartment, and know that I have no reason to getup the next day. I don't want to be alone anymore." He pulled in a breath. Going back to that life, now that he'd dared to try again, made it almost worse than it had been the first time around.

"But I do want one thing," he said, looking her square

in the eye. This was it. It all came down to this moment. She could take him or leave him. Tell him to go home. Not long ago he wouldn't have even come this far. He had to go for it.

"What's that?" she said.

"You, Bridget. I want you."

*

Bridget knew the music could be playing, or it could have stopped. A toast might be being made, or everyone at the party may have gone home. She didn't notice any of it. All she could see right now was Jack, and the way he was looking at her, and remember every word of what he'd said. Then…and now.

He held out a glass of champagne to her. "What do you say we start over, right from the beginning?"

"And how would that go?" she asked. She needed to know. She needed to be sure this time.

"You're asking J.R. Anderson how the story would end?" He grinned.

She swallowed hard. "I'm asking you."

He nodded, and set the glasses down on the nearest table. "I can't tell you that. That's the scary part. It's…what's kept me from trying again, and it's what almost cost me this." He reached down, took her hand, and against all her reservations, she let him take it.

"So no promises then," she said, but she couldn't fight the smile that was forming when he took a step forward, reaching for her other hand, his gaze never leaving hers.

"Just one," he said, pulling her to give her a long, slow kiss.

Her heart was beating fast when they broke away, looking up into his dark, intense eyes that didn't show any sign of looking away. "What's that?" she asked, but she had a feeling that one promise was all she needed.

He grinned as he pressed her against him. "I never start a story I don't end up finishing," he said. "It may get rocky, it may even feel stalled at times, but I see things through. And I'm here to stay."

"I always knew this town would grow on you," she said through her happy tears.

"You grew on me," he whispered, as he leaned in to kiss her one more time, just as the music swelled.

OLIVIA MILES writes feel-good women's fiction and heartwarming contemporary romance that is best known for her quirky side characters and charming small town settings. She lives just outside Chicago with her husband, young daughter, and two ridiculously pampered pups.

Olivia loves connecting with readers. Please visit her website at www.OliviaMilesBooks.com to learn more.

Made in the USA
Middletown, DE
14 March 2018